Andrew Cull is an award-winning writer and horror director. He wrote and directed the horror hit "The Possession of David O'Reilly." His story collection Bones was released to acclaim in 2018. It has been described as 'a masterclass in emotional cinematic horror fiction.' Andrew lives in Melbourne, Australia. He loves horror and Hitchcock, and, like you, he's not easily scared. Remains is Andrew's debut novel.

REMAINS

By
Andrew Cull

This is a work of fiction. The events and characters portrayed herein are imaginary and are not intended to refer to specific places, events or living persons. The opinions expressed in this manuscript are solely the opinions of the author and do not necessarily represent the opinions of the publisher.

IFWG Publishing International
Melbourne

www.ifwgpublishing.com

Acknowledgements

Thanks to Kerrie, Gerry Huntman, Noel Osualdini, Rebecca Fraser, Steve Dillon, Steve Stred, Luke Newnes, BP Gregory. Your help and support is massively appreciated.

Clifford Cull
1947-2016

I couldn't have done this
without you, Dad.

Foreword

Remains is a work of fiction, but its story is loosely based on recorded events. During the winter of 1974 a series of séances took place in a house in the Bernal Heights district of San Francisco. Over the course of these séances a young mother claimed to have contacted the son she had recently lost in a car accident. However, the messages she received, both by using a Ouija board, and later through a spiritualist medium, alarmed her to such an extent that she contacted a local priest for help. After the séances had taken place, the woman claimed to have felt that something unseen was following her around her home and, more disturbingly, that at night shadows massed around her bed and attempted to choke her. When an exorcism at the house failed to yield any respite in the haunting, the woman contacted a British paranormal investigator and friend of our family who would, many years later, relay the story to me.

While many of the events of that winter could be attributed to a mother's grief (she was later committed to a psychiatric hospital), the messages she received while conducting the séances were so disturbing that they stayed with our family friend long after his investigation had ended. He first told me the story in 2004 when we were discussing another investigation of his that I wanted to adapt into a feature. I've read and heard many ghost stories, many from surprisingly credible sources, but this one has haunted me more than any other. In 2010, after I'd finished shooting my feature, *The Possession Of David O'Reilly*, I was able to travel to San Francisco and visit the house where the séances took place. It's a rented property now, but I was able to get a brief tour from the tenants at the time. That same evening, after visiting the real *1428 Montgomery*, I wrote a feature treatment for a project that would, a few years later, become this novel.

Andrew Cull, Melbourne, 2017

WaTCH you sLEEP

PART ONE

GRIEF IS A BLACK HOUSE

1

No one talked openly about the space, the empty corner of Lucy Campbell's room. The way it would draw your attention, like a stranger quietly whispering your name. The way it was filled with a cold that felt as if it moved over you, pulling the warmth from your body, like someone pulling in a breath before a scream. In the day, the nurses would make their rounds, spending as little time in Lucy's room as possible. At night they left her alone, her muffled sobbing not reason enough to brave *that room* after dark.

For six months, the remains of Lucy Campbell had occupied Room 23b at the William Tuke Psychiatric Hospital, just a freeze-frame of the person she'd been nine months before.

This morning, the ghost of Lucy Campbell stood looking into the thin mirror in her room. Like the rest of Lucy's room, the mirror was old but functional, from the bed that she didn't sleep in, through to the painted white table and chair set by the window that she didn't look out of. This morning Lucy looked into the mirror, but she didn't see herself. Nor did she hear the shrill laugh of the woman in 23a, or the wheelchair clack-clacking across the tiled floor outside her room. A long time ago, Lucy had muted the world around her, fallen deep into herself in an attempt to escape her pain.

At 6:00am, a nurse had left a trolley outside Lucy's room for her luggage. Three of its wheels touched the ground. On to it, Lucy had loaded her two suitcases, one containing her clothes and the other, smaller, the size you might give to a child. The fourth wheel spun in the air as she wheeled her luggage through the maze of corridors towards Reception. The sounds of the busy hospital were dim to Lucy, like a radio playing in another room.

Someone said "Goodbye" and wished her luck. She didn't notice.

The light streaming in through the large glass reception doors was blinding. Lucy stopped. She hung back on the edge of the room, the last refuge of shadows, her dark eyes squinting, searching her mind for something to distract her. She remembered how Doctor Bachman had once complained to her that the board of directors had wasted all the hospital's funding on this flashy reception area.

"We're a hospital, not a bank!" he'd fumed.

Truth was, most of the patients' families didn't want to look any further than the highly polished chrome and glass. They didn't want to know what happened any deeper into the building, and the appearance of affluence afforded them some comfort: they'd made the right decision, their loved ones were in good hands, they could go home with a clear conscience.

Lucy wasn't going home.

The light hurt her eyes. It seemed to be growing brighter all the time, burning away the shadows that sheltered her. She stepped back—with a loud gasp the glass entrance doors slid open, jolting Lucy from her thoughts. A taxi driver had been waiting outside. He tried to take the trolley for Lucy but she held it tight. Pushing it awkwardly between them, they made their way across Reception. Lucy knew she had to do this, had to force herself to do this, it was time; but she couldn't concentrate, couldn't find another memory, another thought to protect herself, and when the automatic doors burst open once more she was defenceless.

"Mommy!" The little boy yelled. Lucy spun to the voice. For a moment she was alive again. The boy laughed, dodging in and out of the trees in the park across from the hospital. His mother sprang from behind a large pine, growling, the monster in their game, and the little boy squealed with glee and raced away. Lucy watched the two playing.

Hold on, Lucy, hold on. She closed her eyes.

Doctor Bachman watched Lucy from the hospital steps. She seemed to physically shrink. *Hold on, Lucy,* he thought, *hold on.*

When Lucy opened her eyes again, the boy and his mother had gone, the taxi driver had loaded her clothes into the trunk and she was gripping the child's size case with white knuckles. Gently, she placed it next to her case.

"Are you sure I can't change your mind?" Doctor Bachman smiled warmly. He polished his thick glasses on his shirt. That was his tell. He always did that when he was worried. He would have made a terrible poker player.

"It's too soon, Lucy. After what you've been through, you need to give yourself more time." Lucy could hear the quiet, fatherly concern in his voice. "We've made good progress, but you should give it another month, or two."

For six months, Doctor Bachman had held Lucy back from the brink, but now she couldn't explain to him why, without warning, yesterday she'd discharged herself from his care. Lucy got into the cab.

"At least do me a favour then…" Doctor Bachman fumbled in his shirt pocket and pulled out a crumpled business card. "Here… Call me with your details, where you're staying, a phone number. And call me if you need to talk about it. Please. You know you can come back at any time."

Lucy took Doctor Bachman's card. The taxi began to pull away.

"Take care, Lucy." Doctor Bachman followed the cab as it made its way up the hospital's drive towards the main gates.

Don't go back to that house, Lucy. Whatever you do, don't go back to that house.

2

The small green door was down a flight of steps off Berkeley. Lucy and the taxi driver parted ways in as awkward a fashion as had characterized their whole brief journey together. She paid him and he unloaded the larger of her two cases onto the sidewalk. Lucy unloaded the smaller case herself. It only occurred to the driver once he'd left that Lucy hadn't spoken a single word the entire trip. The hospital had provided the address, and when she'd come to pay the forty-dollar fare, she'd simply handed him a fifty and got out of the cab. She'd headed around to the trunk of the car and waited, silently. He could sense her anxiety, which only abated when she had the small case in her hands once more. He'd driven a lot of strange people in his time, but never someone as consumed by sadness as her.

It had begun to rain. Pulling her coat over the small case to protect it, Lucy climbed down the stairs to the basement flat. She unlocked the green door to the green apartment, spreading a wave of junk mail across the hallway floor as she pressed the door open. No one had lived here for some time.

Even with the blinds open, the basement apartment was dark. Labelled packing boxes, long since covered in a thick layer of dust, had been placed in their corresponding rooms. Lucy brushed past two boxes, *LIVING ROOM*, as she moved through the gloom. None of the boxes had been touched, as if the last tenant had simply vanished before they'd had a chance to unpack. Lucy pushed open a door at the back of the living room. A breath of stale air escaped the room. The door came to rest, knock-knocking against another full box, *BEDROOM*. Lucy gently laid the small case on the bed. For a long moment she thought about opening it, her fingers close, almost touching the catches. *Not now*. She dropped her hand away and backed out of the bedroom. Without taking her eyes from the case, Lucy gently pulled the door closed. Outside, Lucy's other case sat abandoned in the rain.

The next morning the rain had turned to ice. Early commuters, sucking in the freezing air between sips of *Starbucks*, paced along Berkeley. Wrapped tight against the San Francisco winter, two beat cops, nearing the end of their tour, laughed about what they'd seen last night. Holding the rail, the mailman gingerly made his way down the frozen steps to Lucy's green door. More junk mail to add to the pile that Lucy hadn't cleared, and a large letter that the mailman had to roll to fit through the slot. Unfurling on top of the junk pile, the ivory envelope addressed to *MRS LUCY CAMPBELL* had been dispatched the previous day from the law firm Sage and Kingsbury.

Just a few feet from the bustling beginning of a San Francisco day, a deep, mournful silence filled Lucy's apartment, as if the sadness she carried with her had spread into the very dust that choked the air. Lucy had begun to unpack the two boxes marked *LIVING ROOM*. She'd scattered a few books across the shelves, and ornaments sat on the protective newspaper they'd travelled in, unwrapped but homeless. On top of one of the boxes, a photograph lay half unwrapped. Lucy beamed from between the folds of newspaper, a broad, beautiful smile, captured on Alex's sixth birthday. Her son and her husband—her world. They'd laughed so hard at Matt's attempts to get the timer on his camera to work. He'd taken shots of his back, of him startled when the shutter had triggered too soon, of the three of them cracking up when they thought it wouldn't trigger at all. In the end, he'd just held the camera as far away as his arm allowed. From a photographer's perspective it was a terrible shot, but it had been Lucy's favorite for a long time. If she'd remembered it was in that box, she would never have started to unpack it. Abandoned as soon as she realized what she was holding, torn newspaper still obscured Alex's face.

In the kitchen, the kettle on the stove began to whistle. Lucy had made up the small dining table for one. Popped toast sat in the toaster, long since cold. Lucy stood against the workbench holding a small plate tightly, her whole body tense, fighting. A tear fell onto the plate in her hands. The sound of the kettle built to a scream, loud enough to drown out the single sob that escaped her clenched jaw. She brought a hand to her mouth. To force the pain to stay inside, stay silent. There was so little of the Lucy from that photograph left that it would be easy for the last of her to be consumed by her grief, to be swallowed forever by the darkness that was always at her back.

Today was the first day of Lucy's *new* life.

3

Doctor Bachman stood in the hallway of the William Tuke Psychiatric Hospital looking at the neat stacks of care packages. Each month the children of the Sacred Heart Catholic School would pack thirty-three shoe boxes with dried fruit, warm clothing, books, everything they felt the patients might need to make their lives a little better. Then, each month, on the first Saturday of the month, Sister Catherine would drop the packages off, neatly stacking them in six piles, three of six and three of five in the hallway by the common room. Doctor Bachman guessed that Sister Catherine must have been in her late sixties but she never asked for, or accepted, any help when she was delivering the boxes. She carried every one, every month, to build the same neat stacks.

Doctor Bachman lifted the lid on the top box in stack three. Resting on top of the other donations was a thin copy of the Bible. Doctor Bachman took out the Bible and started a new pile of boxes.

Half an hour later and Doctor Bachman made his way into the patient's day room, balancing a stack of thirty-three Bibles. In the middle of the room, surrounded by sagging couches, a coffee table had been covered with magazines and books. Doctor Bachman dropped a single Bible onto the table.

"One's enough."

Peeking around the stack of thirty-two remaining Bibles, Doctor Bachman headed out of the common room and back up the corridor towards his office. For some time it had been Doctor Bachman's policy to put a name plaque on the door of each patient's room, next to their room number. He didn't want them to see themselves as numbers. Ted Rubin waved to Doctor Bachman as he passed his room. Ted was forty-five.

He'd lived at the hospital for the last fourteen years. He had good months and bad months. At one time he'd become unresponsive for so long that they had to put him on a drip to feed him. For the best part of a week, Doctor Bachman barely left his side in the infirmary.

As he reached 23b, Doctor Bachman smiled. A shadow moved across the frosted glass window in Lucy's door. He pushed the door open. "I knew you wouldn't..."

Doctor Bachman's words trailed off. Lucy's room was empty. Disappointed, he placed the stack of Bibles onto the recently stripped mattress of Lucy's old bed. He was annoyed with himself. He shouldn't have let her go. She wasn't ready to face the world again yet. He also knew there was nothing he could have done to stop her. Lucy had checked herself in voluntarily six months ago. There was no treatment order keeping her at the hospital. She was free to leave at any time. That didn't stop him from feeling like he'd failed her.

Doctor Bachman took off his glasses. He stood in the window of 23b looking out onto the hospital's frozen grounds. He hadn't realized he was doing it but he'd begun to polish his glasses on his shirt again. A movement behind him caught his attention.

Doctor Bachman turned and looked into the corner of the room. There was nothing there, just as there had been no one there when he'd stepped into Lucy's room. Maybe it was a change in the light, a cloud passing over the sun that had tricked him. It had certainly grown darker. And quieter. And that unnerved him. It was rare, even in the middle of the night, for the hospital to be completely soundless but, as Doctor Bachman's gaze was drawn into the corner, focussed into the seemingly empty space, the hospital had fallen silent. No, that wasn't right. The noise hadn't stopped. It had been *smothered*.

Nurse Bradley's voice startled him.

"There you are, Doctor. I've got the paperwork here to release this room. I just need you to sign it for me." She held the forms out towards him.

Doctor Bachman steadied himself. "Not yet, Mary. Not yet." He wasn't ready to give up on Lucy.

Nurse Bradley folded the forms and pocketed them. She shivered. "We should get someone to look at the heating before we put anyone else in here. It's absolutely freezing."

She left the Doctor to his contemplation. His attention returned to the corner of Lucy's room. Mary was right. It was freezing in 23b. Maybe there was a window open, a draught. That would explain the Bibles. How the neat stack of thirty-two Bibles that Doctor Bachman had placed on the bed had come to be scattered across the mattress.

No windows were open.

4

Lizzie Morgan had given Lucy a tour of the Chronicle with one eye constantly fixed on the glass-walled office in the corner of the room. Even when they'd left the main newsroom, toured the corridors and passed through the staff lounge, she'd continually glanced in the direction of that fishbowl room, as if she could somehow see through the walls that obscured her view, to check her email or see if extension 225 was ringing.

"You can access everything from the past twenty years on the intranet; I'll get IT to buzz you and set up your password for that. Anything older than twenty years, and I'm afraid it's a trip to the basement and the archive. Which—"

Throughout the tour Lizzie had cradled a battered card folder, full to the point of having begun to split, under her arm. It was so full that someone had tied what appeared to be a long shoe lace around its middle in an attempt to stop its sides from tearing any further.

"—is exactly where your first job's going to take you. Mal Anderson wants everything we've got on the Zodiac case. He's leading on Sunday with an alternate theory of the case and he's gonna need everything we ran at the time on his desk by tomorrow morning at the latest."

A light flickered to life on the phone on Lizzie's desk. Before the phone had even begun to ring she was backing away from Lucy. The tour was over.

"Er… He's also made some more specific notes he wants checked in the front of that folder," she called back, her voice getting louder as she strode further away. As the glass doors to Lizzie's office closed behind her, she shouted back: "You need anything else, my extension's 225."

Lucy looked down at the battered folder in her hands. She pulled on the shoelace, untying it. The folder sighed, breathing out, the thick pages crammed inside shifting, pressing at its sides until they threatened to burst. All around her, the office buzzed and spun in a state of constant movement and change. Like the pieces of a puzzle that would never be solved. Noise piled on top of noise, louder, louder, the whole room competing to be heard at once.

Silence. The soundless corridor put Lucy on edge. Coming from the overwhelming noise of the Chronicle's newsroom, it felt out of place, almost surreal. As if stepping through the door from the Chronicle had transported her to some mute, alien realm. Lucy felt her skin prickle. She looked up and down the windowless, grey corridor. She was completely alone.

Trying to hold Mal Anderson's disintegrating folder together, Lucy made her way along the corridor towards the elevator.

An ajar door that should have led to the welcoming offices of a portrait photographer now led only into darkness. Abandoned, like so many offices after the financial crash, prints and paperwork had been scattered across the floor. A telephone cord, picked out by the light from the corridor, the shattered smile of a broken advertising board… A giant eye seemed to follow Lucy as she passed.

Lucy pressed the elevator's call button.

Nothing.

Something had shifted in the atmosphere in the corridor. Lucy suddenly felt absolutely certain that someone else was going to appear in the hallway at any moment. Maybe pulling themselves from one of the dark offices, or by tearing around the corner at either end of the corridor. Either way, she felt they were approaching fast, rushing towards her. Lucy hit the call button again.

And then a third time. Harder.

Still nothing.

She looked for a sign to the stairwell. She could feel her body tightening, getting ready to bolt. Loudly, above her, the elevator's cables snapped taut and it began to grind and creak its descent towards her floor.

As soon as the doors were wide enough for her to pass through, Lucy slipped between them. She found the button for the basement and hit it. Once, twice… The elevator doors continued to open. Three, four times. *Come on! Come on!* The doors locked at their widest point. The silence returned. And with it, the ever-growing sense that something was coming. Lucy backed up until she felt the cold metal of the elevator's wall pressing into her spine. Still the doors remained wide open.

She had to get out of there. She forced herself forward, inching across the stained steel floor, straining to see around the edges of the car. Her anxiety had grown to real fear now. Fear that had wrapped its black arms tightly around her chest, squeezing her lungs, making it hard to catch her breath. Lucy took another tentative step forward. The heavy doors jerked backwards, bucking against their rails, before finally starting to slowly close. The corridor shrank until it was only a glimpse, and then it was gone. Lucy's stomach turned over as the elevator sank towards the basement.

She tried to calm down; convince herself it was all in her head. Like she'd done in the hospital, like Doctor Bachman had taught her, she searched for a memory, an image to cling to, but all she found inside herself was darkness.

An unmanned CCTV camera covered the elevator. The camera recorded Lucy pacing by the door at the front of the car. It also recorded the deep shadow that stretched across the rear of the elevator.

Lucy focussed on the discolored, numbered lights blinking on and blinking out as each floor passed. Eventually the elevator came to a stop. She waited for the doors to open. She could feel her chest tightening again. The cold that she'd felt at the back of the elevator had stretched forward to find her.

And then the doors began to part. Lucy barged through the gap, slamming her shoulder into the opening door with such force that it almost tore Mal Anderson's folder from her hands. Without stopping or looking back, she hurried into the basement archive.

Behind her, the elevator doors yawned wide. Once more they locked open, motors grinding, tightening, before angrily jolting back and finally beginning to close. This time, however, just before the doors were about to meet, they stopped. A foot or so away from closing, the doors froze and then quickly retreated.

The pool of shadow that spread across the back of the elevator car seemed to have grown darker, thicker.

After a long moment, the doors began to close once more. This time they met, metal pressing against metal, locking tight. Whatever they had caught on last time had gone.

5

N ow Lucy could breathe, and she breathed deeply. She filled her lungs
with the comforting smell—her university library, summer days in
the attic of the house she grew up in, the hazy smell of afternoons spent
hunting through boxes filled with the imagined mystery of her parents'
past, stories of intrigue and romance—where her parents were played by
Cary Grant and Grace Kelly—invented from props she plucked from the
dusty storage crates. Those stories always ended the same way, after the
shipwreck, after the cliff top car chase, after the credits had rolled, with
Lucy, content, dressed in a dusty costume she'd scavenged, reading a book
and snacking on the plate of peeled carrots that her father would leave by
the loft hatch for her. Brain rations for adventurers, he called them, snuck
away from Mom's Sunday dinner preparations.

Recently, Lucy had taken comfort in the thought that one day soon she
might come to an end, lie down and simply stop, silent and wrapped in the
warm, safe scent of the past.

The San Francisco Chronicle archive is huge: a vast, rambling under-
ground library housing over one hundred years of San Francisco history.
The work of four generations of reporters. Every important event
witnessed and documented. Typed up, sketched down, scrawled on
everything from notepads to napkins, library stacks stuffed ceiling high
with boxes ordered by year and month. In reverent silence, Lucy made
her way through the archive until she came to a series of stacks labelled
1967-1969.

Lucy continued on, another ten or so years deeper, until she came
to a bank of desks. Eight desks. All eight were empty. At one time, the

archive had been the beating heart of the Chronicle. Now it was rare for three people to visit in a week. Lucy took a desk facing back the way she'd come. She didn't feel comfortable with her back to the elevator. She gently placed Mal Anderson's folder down and flicked on the desk lamp. Dust swarmed in its beam, stirring and settling, drawn to the monitor of the research terminal perched at the back of the desk.

As careful as she'd tried to be, Mal Anderson's folder wasn't going to be leaving the archive again. Its sides had finally torn open and the bulging contents spilled across the desk. Lucy looked down at the pages of notes, research, crime scene photographs. It wasn't the first time she'd seen such graphic images. David Faraday shot in the back of the head, Betty Lou Jensen's body wrapped in a blanket, shot five times in the back trying to flee from the Zodiac. David was seventeen, she was only sixteen. Two children slaughtered like animals.

Lucy pulled Mal Anderson's scribbled notes over the crime scene photographs. Her hands were shaking, she tried to breathe deeply the reassuring smell of the archive, to take herself back to the safety of her attic room, but now that room was covered in blood. The blood of a child. Did they call out before they died? Did they scream out for help but no one came? *Why didn't you do something, Lucy? Anything?* Lucy stood up fast, her chair screeching across the tiled floor. She stepped away from the desk, and then stopped and grabbed a hold of the chair to steady herself.

Aisle *1967 to 1969* was closed, the stacks on rails rolled together. Lucy looked up aisle *1970 to 1973*, checking it was clear before taking hold of the large wheel at the end of the rack. The weight of the moving stack could easily crush someone caught in its path. She gripped the wheel. The unit was heavy, the wheel hard to turn, but eventually the stack began to shift, slowly rolling towards *1973*, opening up the aisle Lucy needed.

With every turn of the wheel the aisle next to Lucy grew slimmer until *1970* came to rest on *1973*, the heavy units knocking against one another. Reading from Mal Anderson's list, Lucy headed into the passageway she'd just made. 1967 took up the first half of the stack to her right, floor to ceiling archive boxes, different sizes, different colours, different states of disrepair. May and June were water-stained and warped, likely casualties of the flood of '88. The smell of mould grew stronger as Lucy headed deeper between the stacks.

December 1968 perched high on the last shelf, at the farthest point of the aisle. It was probably the heaviest box, too. A lifetime ago she would have found that amusing.

Lucy brushed the box with her fingertips. Standing on tiptoes, she was able to push it so a corner hung over the edge of the shelf. She tried to lift the box, get her hand underneath it, but it was too heavy. Lucy put a foot onto the bottom shelf, then pulled herself up onto the unit. Her movement muffled the quiet knocking that had begun at the end of the stack.

Both feet off the ground now, Lucy eased *December 1968* further off the shelf. The knocking grew louder. The unit shifted on the tiles. The aisle shrank a little. Then a moment later, the stack rocked back into place. Lucy managed to get a hand underneath the box. She was going to have to pull it until it began to tip, and then catch it. The knocking came again. The stack inched into the aisle in time with the sound.

Lucy grabbed a hold of the shelf. She felt that. She felt the unit shift. She looked back to the end of the stack. And that was when she saw it.

Was someone there? Peering around the end of the aisle? She was sure she'd glimpsed someone—a shape. Lucy stepped down onto the tiles. The knocking came again. Again the wall of archive boxes shifted towards her. Cautiously, Lucy headed towards the noise.

She found herself hugging the huge stack, pressing into it as if she were hiding behind a giant for protection. She could feel each knock vibrating through the stack. The unit rocked forward, rocked back in time with the sound. With each knock, with each step she took, the sense that something terrible awaited her grew.

But Lucy couldn't stop. She was being drawn along the aisle. Not by fear or by some dark curiosity, but something else, something inside her, something that tethered her, pulled her towards whatever lurked ahead. As she passed the water-damaged boxes, the smell of rot caught in her throat. It hadn't been that strong before, had it? It hadn't filled the whole aisle. Soon the stack would run out, the giant would step away, and Lucy would be left completely alone.

The knocking grew faster, louder. She strained to see into the corridor but the stacks had her blocked on both sides. The fear that had unfurled in her stomach flared into panic. Then Lucy was at the end of the aisle.

The instant she stepped into the corridor, the knocking stopped. The wheel handle on the stack rolled backwards and locked, as if someone who was part-way through turning it had just let go. Could someone have been here? Just a moment ago? Lucy looked along the corridor, following the rows of stacks towards the double entrance doors and then back towards the bank of desks, and then she froze.

Certain that any noise she made would muffle the approach of the dark shape she'd glimpsed, she stood absolutely still, listening. The silence of the archive pressed in her ears: charged.

Lucy stood at the end of aisle *1967 to 1969* for ten minutes more before she worked up the nerve to turn her back on the corridor. *December 1968* stuck out awkwardly, half on and half off of the shelf.

Lucy pressed the box against her stomach and leaned backwards. Her arms ached from its weight. The corrugated card around the box's handles had started to cut off the blood to her fingers. As she walked quickly back to the desk where she'd left Mal Anderson's notes, she looked down each aisle leading off from the corridor. With every glance she expected to see the shape, pressed into the shadows against one of the stacks, biding its time. There were many places to hide in the archive.

By the time she made it back to the desk she was losing the battle to hold on to the box. She dropped it with a thud that made the research terminal's mouse jump and the monitor at the back of the desk blink on.

With a startled gasp, Lucy recoiled from the image on the screen. The house. That terrible black house. How did it get there? Who did this? A headline above the image read: BOY SLAIN IN KIDNAP GONE WRONG.

Somewhere close by, a child laughed.

6

And Lucy laughed too.

"Hi! You're through to the Campbell Clan," Lucy's voice called out to the shadows and dust in her deserted apartment.

"I'm afraid that Lucy, Matt, and Alex aren't here right now, so please leave us a message after the beep..."

Giggling, Alex beeped and then he was gone, snatched back into memory as the recording ran out. The real beep followed and Lucy's machine began to record.

No one spoke. Outside on Berkeley, the first office workers were leaving for the evening, their shadows stretching after them, following them home. Long, dark fingers reaching across Lucy's apartment as they crossed the small window in her kitchen. Still no message came.

It was indistinct at first—distant—more of a shift in the pitch of the silence at the other end of the line. Something moved. Quickly muffled by the thick quiet, it was easy to miss. The second movement was clearer.

At the other end of the line, something dragged itself closer. Dipping in and out of the hush, each time the noise came it was louder, nearer.

Inch by inch, raw and sticky, it gained on Lucy's answering machine. The darkness in Lucy's apartment had swelled. Pooling in the lounge as if it were bleeding from the place at the other end of the open line, leading the way for whatever pulled itself ever closer.

The line abruptly cut off, Lucy's machine reaching its maximum recording time and severing the connection. The apartment fell silent once more. Whatever lurked in the thick black would remain there a while longer.

The same silence filled the archive. Lucy had left the box of papers where she'd dropped it, caught in 1428 Montgomery's unflinching stare. The shot, taken in the early hours of the morning after, had come to represent the end of Lucy's world. An ambulance swung up onto the lawn, the horror and confusion written across Detective Bob Taylor's face. At the time, Lucy hadn't even known what had happened yet.

In the archive there are eight research terminals. In the dying light of the day, eight research terminals displayed a single image: the house.

7

Three hours earlier.

Rising over the brow of the hill, brick by brick, floor by floor, as if it were hauling itself from the earth beneath, 1428 Montgomery came into view. Lucy pulled into the curb and shut off the engine. She sat, one hand on the key in the ignition, watching the house.

The house watched back.

She knew she shouldn't be here. She also knew it was inevitable that she would end up here. Without removing the keys, Lucy's hand dropped away from the ignition. The first day of her new life was going to end the same way each long day of her life before the hospital had ended.

For three hours she sat silently watching 1428 Montgomery. As the afternoon turned to evening, darkness stretched from the house, its giant shadow spilling out across the overgrown lawn towards Lucy. Nine months ago, someone had driven a *For Sale* sign, like a stake, into the lawn. If they had meant to kill the darkness, they'd failed. With each minute it grew, reaching ever closer to Lucy's car.

Lucy opened her mouth to speak but no words came out. She spoke so little recently that she barely recognized her own quiet voice when she heard it. She thought it sounded like the voice of a ghost. After the murder, she'd come to realize that there was little point in speaking any more. There wasn't anything left to be said. There wasn't anyone left that she wanted to speak to. Her voice had withered away and died. She tried again,

"Doctor Bachman says I shouldn't come here." Her words were barely a whisper. "Well, where else am I supposed to go?"

Lucy looked away from the house. She'd thought about this conversation, thought about how she'd explain. She'd played it out in her head, night after night in the hospital. Now she didn't know what to say.

"I know I've been away for a while. I'm sorry about that. I... er... I've not been very well. Don't worry, though. It's okay. I'm better now. I still thought about you every day. I think about you every minute of every day."

Her words caught in her throat, sadness stealing what little voice she'd mustered. She sat for a minute before she could go on. Outside, the shadow of the house had reached Lucy's car.

"When I was staying at the hospital there was a lady who, every month, delivered shoe boxes, care packages, to everyone on my ward. Over thirty boxes filled with books, clothes, sweets made by the congregation of her church."

Lucy talked to the house, talked to Alex.

"It was a decent thing to do, a kind thing, but at the top of every box—the first thing you saw when you opened it—she always put a Bible. Like one of those free ones you get when you stay in a cheap hotel."

The tone of Lucy's words had changed, as if the darkness that stretched over her car had somehow found its way into her lungs. Her voice grew stronger.

"It made me so angry that I went through every one of those boxes, I took out every one of her Bibles and I threw them all in the trash. I said to her, 'People can wear your clothes, they can eat your food, but what good are your Bibles to us? What good are lies and false promises to people whose lives have crushed them so badly they had to book themselves into a hospital for the fucking insane?' "

Lucy spat the words. "I told her, 'I know there's no God. I know that, because, if there were, he wouldn't have let my seven-year-old son be kidnapped from outside his house. He wouldn't have let him be terrified and alone with a man...' "

Lucy ground her teeth, unable to stifle the sob that escaped her mouth.

"'...with a man who took a shotgun and pointed it at my son's head...'" She clapped a hand over her mouth, as if stopping her words might somehow stop the terrible thoughts. She felt her tears streak the back of her hand.

Lucy fought to keep herself together for Alex's sake. She hated crying in front of him.

"Oh, Alex. I'd give anything for you to be here now."

The knock on the passenger side window made Lucy start.

She turned away, wiping her eyes, hiding her grief. Her pain was private, between her and her son.

Matt leaned down and knocked again. When she was ready, Lucy wound down the window.

"Are you okay?" Matt asked.

Lucy nodded. Matt could see that was a lie.

"You shouldn't be here," he said.

"Neither should you."

"Doctor Bachman said you'd discharged yourself."

Nothing from Lucy.

"He just called because he's worried about you."

"Is that why you came here?"

Nothing from Matt this time.

Matt watched Lucy. Christ, she was so thin. She'd been in the hospital for six months. He'd expected that she'd look healthier when he saw her next, that all that time away might have helped her, that she might show some signs of recovering. She didn't. She looked frail, beaten. She barely looked at him, instead staring ahead or away to that awful house. How had they come to this?

"Did you get the papers?" He placed a hand on the half-wound window. Lucy noticed he was still wearing his wedding ring. "There's no hurry for you to sign them."

Matt followed Lucy's gaze up to 1428 Montgomery. For a long time the husband and wife watched the house without speaking, a facade of white clapboards and somewhere, in its heart, the blood of their son. The family who'd lived there had been away that night. No one knew what had drawn the kidnapper to take Alex to that house.

"Do you think it ever gets any easier?" Lucy could hear the pain in Matt's voice. She wanted to comfort him, but stayed looking up to the house.

Matt took a piece of paper from his pocket. "I've…er…got a new number. Here." He handed to it Lucy. "You can call me, if you want. Any time."

Lucy took the note. A year ago they'd been a family, shared everything. "Are you going to be okay?" He wanted to say much more.

"No. I don't think it ever gets any easier," Lucy said.

The house watched Matt as he returned to his car, like a child watching ants on the sidewalk.

8

5:00am.

Lucy had spilt the bottle of sleeping pills. She'd been drunk when she'd read the divorce papers. She hadn't signed them.

She'd stayed at the house until she couldn't stand the silence any longer. Then she'd stopped off at a liquor store on the way back to her apartment. She hadn't waited till she was home to open the bottle.

Lucy's answering machine blinked in the dark. A lone buoy in the sea of shifting shadows that haunted the monochrome apartment. There had been a time when Lucy had taken to sleeping with the lights on. Less places for the ghosts to hide. But then they'd started creeping into the light, and she'd stopped sleeping altogether.

Lucy lay on the bed, her still eyes staring ahead, seeing nothing. The small case lay at her side, her arm draped over it, hugging it to her. She'd taken enough of the pills to fell a man twice her size.

She'd thought about suicide before. Not straight after Alex's death, but as time drew on and the unbearable emptiness left by his murder had consumed her. She knew there was nothing waiting, no tunnel to a better place, no comfort to be found in the lies other people told themselves. She'd been in that better place: her home every single day that Alex had been alive. Then *he* had taken a shotgun, placed it against her son's head... When she slept, the dream was always the same.

It was dusk at the park, the trees grew taller, their shadows longer, draining the bright colors from the climbing frame and swings. Lucy sat on the bench, its cracked paint pinching at the backs of her bare arms when she moved. She sat forward. She'd waited for hours, and now it was time to leave. Sometimes Lucy would briefly wake at this point, hitting reality like she was drowning, gasping for air before the current could drag her under again. She felt like she was screaming, thrashing to snap herself awake. But in her dream she slowly got up from the bench and headed towards the tunnel.

The broken boy lived in the underpass, somewhere in the shadows. He was small, able to press himself against the walls, into the large cracks in the concrete, to hide in plain sight. His coat was padded, hooded and dirty. His hood was soaked with blood.

Lucy stood at the tunnel's entrance. Her legs carried her forward, inevitably forwards, towards him and her dream's terrible conclusion. Somewhere she was fighting to wake herself, terrified and desperate to take control of her body. Here, Lucy stepped ever onwards until the tunnel swallowed her whole.

The ceiling of the tunnel was riddled with cracks, snaking across the concrete like thick veins bulging at the surface of aged, grey skin. Behind Lucy, the light of a dying day lingered sheepishly at the underpass's entrance. Ahead there was no light, no sign of any way out.

The deeper she ventured, the colder the damp air became. It slipped beneath her thin cotton shirt, making her skin pull tight. She hugged herself, trying to stay warm, her breath like a ghost materializing on the air ahead of her. He was here. Somewhere, the broken boy watched her.

Lucy turned fast to look back the way she'd come. This was how the dream always went! He wasn't behind her. He wasn't ever behind her! He was somewhere in front; tiny, bloody hands growing closer all the time.

Her heart was slamming in her chest. She couldn't see the dusk light, the tunnel entrance, *the only way out*, anymore.

Any time now.

Lucy held her hands out in front of her, feeling through the darkness, trying not to stumble, the tunnel, like an ever-developing photograph, forming foot by foot ahead of her.

No! No! No! Any time now she would feel the wet, padded nylon of his jacket. *Please, not again!* She wanted to clench her hands into fists, pull her fingers tight, delay just a moment longer, but the Lucy in the dream never responded to her cries. And then he was there.

Lucy's fingers grazed the fur lining of the boy's hood. She snatched her hand back but he kept coming. He hugged her waist, clinging on tightly. She could feel the blood from his hood soaking into her shirt, cold, sticking to her stomach. She knew that blood was specked with bone. *Please stop, make it stop.* Lucy could feel him shaking. She looked down at the boy. At his misshapen hood pulled up tight, masking the terrible horror to come. She knelt before him.

"It's okay," Lucy whispered gently. The boy turned to look at her. Lucy wanted desperately to look away but her gaze was fixed. As the hood turned, she could see that it was flat on one side. Where the boy's head should have filled the hood, it hung loosely. Bloody and empty.

The boy wrapped his arms around Lucy's neck. He was cold; always so cold. Closer, he leaned in to her until he rested the hood upon her shoulder.

"It's okay," Lucy whispered.

NO! NO! NO! Somewhere, in another world, Lucy screamed for the dream to stop. *Stop now!* She begged, she pleaded, but still she placed her hand on the hood to comfort the boy. As she pressed in to the empty side of the hood, her fingers stuck to the wet material. *Please stop!* But she pressed further, wet fingers pushing, searching deeper for whatever horror lay inside. Lucy could feel the boy's blood spilling from the dark mouth of the hood. It soaked her shirt. Still she pressed, collapsing the empty material. Then she felt it—a weight shifting inside the hood—bone grinding against bone, the last pieces of the boy's skull collapsing at her touch.

Nowadays, Lucy took the sleeping pills because most nights they stopped the dreams. If one day they killed her, it would be a happy accident. She blinked. That day was not today.

Lucy stared into the darkness by her bed. She shivered and pulled her coat closed. The cold had followed her into the bedroom at around 4:00am. It seemed to have settled in the space beside her bed. Now, it pulled at each breath she took, drawing the warm air from her lungs and freezing it, returning it so cold she could feel it hitting her throat. Maybe it was the mix of sleeping pills and booze but the shadows by the side of her bed seemed much thicker than anywhere else in the room.

Lucy stretched out a hand. She reached into the black the way the Lucy in her nightmare had reached for the broken boy. The air felt so cold it seemed to move over her skin. She reached deeper. When her fingers brushed against the lamp on her bedside table, she almost tore her hand away. Now, more than ever, the nightmare haunted her. Cold blood and broken bone, lurking in the gloom her fingers crept through. She found the base of the lamp, ran her hand quickly to the cord and flicked the switch.

The energy-saving bulb blinked on, dim light pressing back the shadows as best it could. Still, it was bright enough to hurt Lucy's eyes. As she turned away, it seemed as if the shadows turned with her, shifting fast on the edge of her peripheral vision.

She closed her eyes. Her world was a sleep-deprived blur. She'd stopped moving but the world still swam inside her head. She didn't trust her senses any more.

Then she felt it.

The cold that had watched her through the night clambered up onto her bed. She felt it move over her feet, crawling up her legs until it came to rest on her chest. She felt its weight, its broken form. She felt it reach into her mouth with her breath and scratch and scrape down her throat.

Lucy's eyes snapped open. The bedroom was still and silent. The weight she'd felt smothering her was gone. The bulb had warmed up, glowing brighter. It had won its battle against the night for now. In another room, Lucy heard the heating fire up. She sighed. Maybe she'd dozed for a moment, the Tamazepam and alcohol finally overcoming her. That didn't explain why her sigh smoked on the air, white and then gone, like a ghost fleeing her lungs. Lucy exhaled again. She couldn't see her breath anymore.

She'd thought about it all night long. The alcohol and sleeping pills couldn't numb or distract her thoughts. Lucy stood over the packing box. Each one of the dust-covered boxes had been labelled: *KITCHEN, LIVING ROOM, BEDROOM*, except one. She ran her fingers along the length of the tape sealing the box, drawing a trail through the dust. She followed with a knife splitting and tearing through the plastic tape.

9

It had pulled itself out of the box. Out of the darkness into the dim light of the green apartment. There it lay, in the silence. Repeated a thousand times, like a desperate prayer.

Lucy's phone began to ring. No one came to answer it. It rang until Lucy's answering machine kicked in. Lucy was nowhere to be found.

The laughter followed, Alex beeped and then there was silence once more.

No one spoke. From the floor, the house on Montgomery watched on. Hundreds of photographs, article after article about Alex's death, thousands of words written about that terrible day.

"Hello? Er, hello?" Doctor Bachman wasn't very good with answering machines. "Lucy... Hi, it's Doctor Bachman here. Matt... er... gave me your number. Just calling to check in really, see how you're getting on."

The box without a label had been full of paper, full of cuttings—every word written on Alex's case that Lucy could find. Before the hospital, she'd begun keeping the reports on Alex's death. She found that she couldn't part with the paper recollections, the mentions of his name. She tore them from newspapers, cut them from magazines. When Mal Anderson had written a four-page special in the *Sunday Chronicle*, she'd driven for miles buying up every copy she could find.

She'd begun hiding them from Matt. She filled drawers, and when the drawers were full of words, of pictures of that black house, she'd moved on to boxes, suitcases, anywhere she could find with space enough to cram her son's name. When she'd arrived at the hospital, her pockets had been stuffed with paper.

"I... er... I'm pretty free for the rest of the week. Why don't you give me a call and we can have some coffee?"

Lucy had read every word written about that night, she'd ringed sentences, phrases, highlighted and collated. She'd worked as a researcher for years, she knew words, knew their power, knew they would lead her to an answer. They always had.

She just had to keep looking.

"Well, you've got my number. Give me a call. And Lucy, I know it's hard, but you should get rid of this answering machine. Buy a new one, record a new message. Take care, Lucy. Bye."

The house had crawled from the box, its image spilling from the table where Lucy had first unpacked her notes, onto the floor. There it lay, in the silence, repeated a thousand times like a curse.

10

The shadows massed outside 1428 Montgomery, squirming and stretching, spreading across the porch. The torch blasted them apart.

"Shhh! Turn it off!" Rod grabbed the torch from Jesse and smothered it with his hand. "Stupid! You want the whole neighbourhood to see us?"

Jesse's eyes could barely get any wider. "Wha... I?" For a moment Rod thought he was going to cry. He handed back the torch. Jesse pulled the sleeve of his red hoodie over the light, muffling it, but not switching it off. Now, everywhere he shone his torch glowed crimson. That didn't make him feel any better at all.

Rod turned to the rest of the shadows. "Right. Are you ready?" He looked at each member of the group in turn, his tone growing increasingly foreboding as he moved along the line. "No, are you *sure* you're ready?"

In the dim light of the dampened torch, three shadows nodded one by one to Rod, their nine-year-old leader. Glen, Rod's best friend, also nine, and joint organizer of this outing, pushed his glasses back up his nose. His mom had made him get these ones on the advice of the optician's assistant, "You'll grow into them," she'd said. "You'll thank me in the long run" That was what his Mom always said when she had no grounding at all for what she was saying. She knew Glen couldn't argue with her though, as "the long run" hadn't happened yet, so how did he know he wouldn't be thanking her when it did? She said it so often he was sure he'd be thanking her for *something* when the time came. He doubted, somehow, it would be for the RSI he'd get from constantly pushing his glasses back up his nose.

Glen nodded he was ready, and turned to Jacob, Rod's seven-year-old brother. Jacob nodded on cue. Next to him, Jesse, also seven, nodded with wide, wide eyes.

Rod looked back to the house, drew in a deep, slow breath, building the atmosphere, and then he began: "It happened in April. Same month as Glen's birthday. There were cop cars all over the street. Isn't that right?"

Glen nodded.

"Glen lives next door, he saw the whole thing. Didn't you?"

Glen nodded; then pushed his glasses back up his nose.

Jesse drew the beam of the red torch across 1428 Montgomery's dark porch. He followed a trail of cracked and peeled paint low across the clapboard-panelled wall until he picked out the legs of a bench. They had one on their porch at home, too. His Mom and Dad spent long summer evenings laughing, drinking and playing cards on theirs.

This bench was nothing like the one they had at home. He wished he was at home now. Resting on bowing beams, a long cushion had rotted, bulging, bloating and finally splitting open. Its innards hung black and wet, dripping into a dark puddle on the deck beneath.

Rod's voice almost set Jesse running. "It took them hours to bring out the bodies. Even the most hardened cops… After they'd seen that room, what he'd done to the kid… They wouldn't go back in there again, couldn't face seeing it again."

Glen nodded.

Jesse moved over the bench with the weak beam of his torch. He pushed the red light into the corners of the bench, around by the back legs, where the darkness was thickest. He imagined seeing a boy curled up between those legs, dead eyes waiting to flicker and find him.

Jesse swung the torch from side to side, from corner to corner of the bench. There was no boy. No dead eyes watched him. He tried to be calm, like the older boys, but he was terrified.

"Eventually they bring out the kid's body. It's covered up on a stretcher. But something's not right. Something's *really* not right. You see, it's too short, even for a seven- year-old's body."

Jacob had begun to follow Jesse's torch, watching its erratic path across the front of the house. It was better than watching Rod.

The torch climbed upwards, finding a large dark window above the bench. Jacob turned to look at Jesse. Even in the dim light he could see how white Jesse had turned. Jacob thought he might bolt, or be sick, at any moment.

Rod stepped into the torch's beam. "You see, that's because the nut who kidnapped him, the freak who snatched him, he took a shotgun…"

Jesse couldn't move. Rod drew closer with each word, the red glow from Jesse's torch lighting up his face, growing more intense with every step. To Jesse he looked like the devil with a buzz cut.

"He took a shotgun and he pressed it against the kid's face." Rod made a gun with two of his fingers. He held it up in front of him, reaching out towards Jesse. Then the devil placed his gun against Jesse's head.

Silence. Glen realized he was holding his breath.

"BANG!!!" Rod pulled the trigger. Everyone jumped. Jacob grabbed a hold of Jesse's arm. Jesse jerked hard against his grip. If he hadn't been holding him he would have run, or worse fallen off of the porch. Jacob held on tight. It wasn't just to stop Jesse. He was terrified, too.

"The nut pulls the trigger…only, only one of the barrels fires." In his panic, Jesse had dropped his torch. The light rolled away across the porch. Now, Rod's words came out of the dark. Without the light to distract them, the boys' imaginations ran wild.

"The shot blows half the kid's head clean off… But it doesn't kill him. It doesn't kill him straight away and he's lying there on the ground, he's screaming, screaming in pain, broken, bleeding, crying out for help."

Jacob put his free hand over his mouth. He still held tightly to Jesse with the other. What Rod described was terrible. Even *his* voice wavered, not quite so certain, not relishing the ghost story quite as much as before.

"The crazy bastard sees what he's done. He takes the shotgun—he can't bear the terrible screaming—and he puts it in his mouth… He closes his eyes and…"

Rod put his fingers to his mouth and shut his eyes.

"BANG!!!"

Glen let out a little scream, followed by: "Shit! Shit, Rod!" as he pulled himself together.

"He unloads the remaining round into his head, blowing his brains all over the walls."

Jesse's wide eyes darted around the porch looking for something to distract him from Rod's story. He stopped on the outline of the black window above the bench. The mottled glass caught a little light from a streetlamp down on the road behind them. Jesse focussed on the glow on the pane. Anything was better than the darkness where his imagination lay screaming and covered in blood.

"That poor kid, lying on the floor, broken, screaming and bleeding. He watched as that monster ate his gun. They said that all night, even after they'd taken the body away, the cops on the scene kept hearing screaming, that terrible screaming. That's right isn't it?"

Glen nodded.

"Glen's heard it. At night, if you listen very quietly, you can hear that horrible screaming."

Rod's voice grew quieter and quieter. He turned to look at the window behind him. The other three friends followed his gaze. For a terrifying moment Jesse thought he saw someone standing in the window. A black shape that moved when Rod moved, mimicking his movements. Rod's reflection gained on the window.

The night had fallen silent, as if the whole neighbourhood leaned close, straining to hear the smallest movement, dreading the sound of the screaming Rod described.

"Right!" Rod's words made all three of his audience start. He whirled around to face Jacob, Jesse and Glen. "Who's first?"

"Wha...?" Jesse couldn't take much more of this.

"The mail slot!"

Glen nodded. Rod had made his way to 1428 Montgomery's front door. Slowly crossing the dark porch, the other three followed.

"The screaming moves from room to room. It moves through the whole house. Glen's heard it, right?"

Glen nodded.

"Sometimes it comes right up to the front door."

Rod listened intently, leaning close, in towards the door. Jesse hadn't been this scared since that night he'd woken from a nightmare and gone downstairs to find his Dad watching *The Shining*. He'd stood in the doorway for ten minutes, watching, eyes as wide as tonight, fascinated and completely terrified until the crazy woman had started screaming, and then he was screaming too.

Rod turned from the door. "Two months ago there's a new mailman. He doesn't know his route yet and he accidentally posts the mail for Glen's house here. It's only after he's done it that he realizes he's got the wrong house. So, he knocks on the door but no-one comes. He looks through the windows. The place looks deserted. He lifts the mail slot—"

They all leaned in as Rod lifted the mail slot (as slow as possible for maximum effect). "And he reaches inside to try and grab back the mail. He's reaching in when he thinks he hears something. Is someone there?"

Jesse realized he was standing right by the rotting bench. He could smell it. His eyes were drawn to the black window once more. Leaning closer, he thought he could make out his own shadow reflected in the dark glass.

Rod continued, "He reaches deeper inside, straining to try and reach the mail." Rod stretched an arm out in front of him, not into the mail slot—he was acting, not crazy! He played his part just like he'd rehearsed it in front of his mirror that afternoon. Rod reached out pretending to grasp for the mail. "He's almost got it when… out of nowhere, a cold hand clamps around his arm!" Rod's other hand tore out of the darkness and clamped around his outstretched arm. Jesse screamed.

"He screams! He's struggling to get away but the freezing hand holds him tight!" Rod played out the struggle to his captivated audience. Glen smiled—this was even better than when Rod had shown him that afternoon.

"Eventually he manages to snap his hand away! He rips his hand out of the mail slot and he runs! He doesn't stop running till he's far away from this place." Rod turned as if he was watching the mailman flee screaming from the house and disappearing into the distance.

When he turned back, his voice was low, almost a whisper as he delivered his final, chilling warning. "If he hadn't managed to get his hand free…God knows what would have happened to him."

Rod reached into his coat pocket. "Safe to say, the next day there was a new mailman on this route!"

He cupped one hand over the other to hide whatever it was he'd just retrieved from his coat. The boys leaned in. What was it? What was Rod hiding in his hands? Rob whipped his cupped hand away to reveal… "Straws!"

Gripped between his thumb and his palm, their lengths hidden from the group, Rod held a line of four glow-in-the-dark drinking straws. He'd found them in the back of the kitchen drawer, left over from last Halloween. What a find! They were perfect for tonight. He'd left them on his windowsill all afternoon to make sure they glowed bright when the time came.

"Who wants to go first?"

Slowly, Rod waved the straws past each of the boys. "Whoever draws the short straw goes first."

"Glen?" As they'd planned, the straws took a slow journey past Glen's face. Rod faked a pause, a false start before heading onwards to Jesse. "Jesse?" Jesse let out a little moan of fear. For a horrible moment, he thought Rod was going to pick him.

"Jacob?" Rod shifted the straws to Jacob. There they lingered, just in front of Jacob's nose. They weren't going anywhere else; Rod had made his choice.

Jacob looked to Glen and Jesse, who watched, transfixed. They didn't want to draw first any more than he did. No one was going to come to his rescue. After a long moment, Jacob reached for the straw furthest to his right.

He changed his mind at the last moment and went far left. Jacob pulled the straw from Rod's hand.

11

"It's short! It's short! You're first!" Rod quickly returned the rest of the straws to his pocket. In truth, all four were equally short, but only he and Glen knew that.

Jacob looked from the straw in his hand to the mail slot. He thought about protesting but that would just make him look like he was scared. He *was* scared—terrified—but he kept quiet.

The front door to 1428 Montgomery was so cold that Jacob was surprised his hand didn't stick to it. It felt like it was coated with ice. Even when he took his hand away, he didn't seem to be able to shake the cold off. It felt like it had eaten into him, somehow fixed inside him. He shivered, looking to Rod in the hope that he'd relent, but Rod just stood watching, waiting…

Reluctantly, Jacob pushed open the mail slot to peer inside.

He wasn't sure exactly what he expected to see on the other side of the freezing door, but all the possibilities he imagined were equally terrible. In truth, he couldn't see very much.

The darkness in the entrance hallway was so thick he couldn't even tell how near or far away anything was. That just made his heart race faster. He leaned close, waiting for his eyes to adjust. He felt cold air on his face, to him the breath of something long dead escaping from the mail slot. Jacob closed his eyes.

"It's only a story," he whispered so the other boys didn't hear.

When he opened his eyes again, they'd begun to grow accustomed to the deep dark. Across the hallway a staircase had materialized. Or, at least, half of one. He followed it step by step upwards with his eyes, until the darkness blocked him from seeing any further. His eyes lingered on the last stair he could make out.

Anyone who goes further than that step will never be seen again, he thought.

Jacob's eyes returned to the hallway. Everywhere he looked, shadows crowded the room—so many places for his nightmares to creep from. Demons eyed him from the darkness, the boy with half a head waited to stretch out his dead arms and grab at him.

"It's only a story," he repeated to himself.

Jacob pulled his sleeve down until it covered his hand. He gripped it from inside with his fist so it wouldn't slip. Something to protect him from whatever lay on the other side of the door. Slowly, he pressed his fist into the slot.

With his hand balled tight it wouldn't pass through the small gap. He tried again, trying to force his covered hand through, get this over with, but all he did was graze his knuckles on the metal surround. Reluctantly he let go of his sleeve, his fingers slipping out from the arm of his sweater. He felt the cold immediately.

It was like reaching into a freezer. Jacob's fingers appeared on the other side of the mail slot, twitching like bait in the water.

"Shh, shh, what was that?" Rod didn't look like he was joking any more. "Shhh! Did you hear that?"

Jacob froze, his hand half through the slot. "What? What?" The boys listened in silence.

Nothing.

The night was completely still.

"I can't hear it now. I…er…I thought."

Jesse was already backing away from the house. "Let's go! Come on. Let's go!"

"No, no! I can do this!"

Jacob's bravery surprised even Rod. He felt sure he'd overplayed his hand just now.

Inside the house, Jacob's hand gradually reached through the mail slot. His fingers became his hand, his hand his wrist.

"I can do this… I can do this…" Maybe if he said it enough times it would be true.

The slot was tight, pushing back Jacob's jacket sleeve as he reached in. His bare arm disappeared deeper into the black.

Outside, his other hand hung forgotten by his side. Rod looked to Glen. Glen nodded. Rod looked into his bag. About twenty minutes before they'd arranged to meet up, while Jacob was having his daily half hour Playstation time, Rod had crept into the kitchen. He'd taken a freezer bag and filled it with ice cubes. Then he'd sealed it and hidden it, wrapped in his scarf, in his bag.

Rod unwrapped the bag. The ice cubes had begun to melt but they'd still do the job. He reached in and grabbed a handful. He was so pleased with his plan that he barely noticed the ice stinging his fingers.

"It's so cold!" Jacob whispered, as if he was worried the screaming boy would hear him. Inside the house, the hairs on Jacob's arm stood up, a last line of defence against the biting air.

Behind Jacob, Rod took his hand from the ice. His fingers hurt now, they throbbed with the cold, but it would all be worth it soon. He began to sneak into position.

Jacob pushed his arm in further still. He was up to his elbow now, almost as far as he could reach. His pale arm stood out against the swarming shadows. Through the window, Jesse thought he saw one of those shadows move.

"It's only a story… It's only a story…"

Rod reached out his icy hand to grab a hold of Jacob's. Inside the hallway, the darkness closed in on Jacob's arm.

Suddenly Jacob started to scream.

12

Thrashing, panicking, trying to tear his arm from the slot, Jacob screamed out, "There's something in there! It's got me! Rod! Help!"

Rod looked to Glen. He hadn't even touched him!

Jesse was gone. He bolted, running, screaming from the porch. Rod just stared. All his bravado gone, he froze, rooted to the spot.

Jacob desperately tried to wrestle his arm from the slot. Crying and shouting for help, he pulled as hard as he could. The metal flap snapped down on his arm, biting into his skin, digging deeper each time he tried to wrench his arm free. Still he fought like his life depended on it.

"Help! Rod! Help!"

Rod wanted to help, he wanted to do something—anything—but he couldn't move, he was just too scared. *Who was that?* Who else was screaming? He could hear it. Underneath Jacob's cries, another voice fighting to be heard.

"Rod! Rod!" This time it was Glen. He rushed forward and jammed his hand into the mail slot. Finding the metal plate, he forced it up and off of Jacob's arm. That should have freed him but still he struggled to get away.

Suddenly, Jacob ripped his bleeding arm clear. The metal plate had peeled back the skin where it had dug into his forearm, but he wasn't feeling any pain. Spinning away from the door, he grabbed Rod by the arm and ran.

Three silhouettes, crying and gasping for breath, hammered through the overgrown front lawn. They didn't look back.

Lucy heard the screaming and got quickly out of her car to investigate. When she saw Jesse—a blur of whimpering terror—race past her and run out into the road, she yelled for him to stop. He didn't even slow down. The next child slammed into her waist.

Turning back, Lucy looked down to see who had run into her. There was no one there. Confused, she looked up just in time to catch a terrified Rod as he tried and failed to dodge around her. She grabbed him, pinning his arms to his sides.

"What are you doing? What's going on?"

She knew she was holding him too tight, shaking him while she was speaking to him, but he'd come from that house and she had to know what had happened.

"There's something! Something in the house! It grabbed Jake!"

"What are you talking about?"

Rod just stared at her, tear-stained and terrified. Lucy relaxed her grip on him. Straight away he wriggled through her fingers and ran.

Lucy looked up to the house. She could feel it urging her forward.

"Are you alright?" Matt's voice called from his car. How long had he been there?

"Why does no one just say 'hi' to me anymore?" Lucy eyed Matt awkwardly trying to lock his car while carrying two cups of takeaway coffee.

"Sorry, hi." He precariously balanced one cup on top of the other.

"Hi."

"What was all that about?" So he had seen her with the boy.

"Just some kids…playing games, I guess"

Matt joined her on the parking strip. He looked up to the house. She could see how it drew his gaze too. In this light Matt looked older than his forty-three years. Lucy didn't remember him having those wrinkles around his eyes. He looked tired.

"What's that?" He'd noticed the copy of *The BFG* she held. It had been one of Alex's favorite books.

"Nothing." Lucy turned back to her car. She threw the book onto the passenger's seat. She planned to follow it, get into the car and leave.

"You want some coffee? I picked some up in case I saw you here."

She could hear the loneliness in Matt's voice. All they had was each other and that black house. Lucy closed the car door and turned back to him. "Okay."

13

Matt's car was still warm, but he switched the heating on all the same. He didn't often have guests these days.

Lucy sipped her coffee. It had been over six months since she'd last sat in this car. It smelt the same as it always had—leather from the seats and oil from the endless weekends Matt had lost under the Camaro's hood. It smelt like the winter they first met.

"How's your new apartment?" It wasn't really new. She'd leased the apartment on Berkley after Matt had found her cuttings. She'd moved out of their house the next day, a voice she'd come to trust whispering it was the only way. A place to store her words, herself, her son. That fractured voice had been her own madness, and less than a month later she'd found herself in the foyer of the William Tuke Psychiatric Hospital, pockets stuffed with paper.

"Green."

Matt couldn't help but tease her. "Really? You hate green."

"I guess I wasn't thinking very straight when I took it."

"Can you paint it?"

"I don't know. I might not stay there long. How about you?"

"It's not green."

"That's nice for you."

For the first time in months a small smile crossed her lips.

Matt had missed that smile.

"I'm sorry I didn't visit you"

Lucy looked out of the window, up to the black panes of 1428 Montgomery. She felt its gaze fixed on her. It was like a third voice, constantly whispering in the background of their conversation.

"Don't be." She turned her back on the house. "The other night, did you come here looking for me?"

Matt thought about lying to her. "No." He knew she'd see right through him, so he told her the truth, or at least a version of it. "I...er... After you went into the hospital I found myself coming here. Once, twice a week, when I couldn't sleep. I don't know why."

Now he was looking past her up to the house. "It makes me sick. I want to smash all its windows. I want to tear it apart, to crush it, grind it into the dirt! I think about it every day. One night I came with a gas can in the trunk. I was going to throw it through a window, light the place on fire, burn it to the ground...but I couldn't do it. I couldn't do it."

Lucy put a hand on Matt's arm.

"And still I keep coming back here. I keep finding myself here." His anger had gone. All that was left was a lonely father who'd lost everything.

"You shouldn't be here," Lucy said gently.

"Neither should you."

They drank the rest of their coffee in silence. In truth they had plenty to talk about—six months of moments when they'd looked to see the other and found only emptiness waiting for them, but the black house had stolen in between them and stifled any further attempts at conversation.

When Lucy had admitted herself to Doctor Bachman's care, Matt had tried to forget her. He'd convinced himself that removing her from his life was the only way he would ever be able to carry on. Not long after she'd gone, the nightmares had started. Then he'd started visiting the house.

Matt finished his coffee. "Will you go home if I do?"

Lucy nodded

"Can we meet somewhere else next time?"

Lucy didn't answer.

"I still make a mean chilli." He'd been wrong. He knew that the moment he saw her again. He'd abandoned her when she'd needed him the most. "How about Friday?"

Lucy wrapped her hands around her empty coffee cup, warming them on its dying heat. After a time she looked up. "Okay."

Matt smiled. "I'll pick you up at seven?"

"Okay."

Cold air swirled into the Camaro as Lucy opened the passenger door and climbed out. She turned and leaned back in, "Go home and get some sleep."

"You too."

Lucy closed the door gently and headed back to her car. Climbing in, she didn't notice that the copy of *The BFG* she'd thrown onto the passenger seat was no longer where it had landed.

Ahead, Matt's Camaro started up. He flashed his lights and pulled away from the curb. Lucy followed him.

It had begun to rain, freezing water drumming on the hood of Lucy's car. The sound had always soothed her. She closed her eyes for a moment, her exhaustion overtaking her. The sound of the rain grew louder, the drumming harder, her wipers arced through the water streaming over her windscreen. Lucy followed Matt for another block.

The lights changed as Matt hit the junction ahead. He made it but Lucy waited, watching Matt's car disappear into the distance. Once he'd gone, she flicked on her indicator. When the light turned green she took a right. She drove two blocks and turned right again. Another block and then right once more.

It was waiting for her.

Welcome back.

Rising up over the brow of the hill, 1428 Montgomery had known she'd return. She'd simply driven around the block so Matt would think she'd gone home. She had no intention of leaving. Not yet. Not tonight.

14

The rain didn't last. Its soothing beat faded and was gone. The whispering of the house took its place. It was always there, under everything else, like a sound you only notice late at night when everything is turned off, when the world is still and dark. Like the sound of electricity, buzzing in overhead lines. Lucy sometimes wondered if she was the only one who heard it. Was it in her head? She felt it in her ears like a change in pressure, gently muffling the world around her, always returning her thoughts back to its dark heart.

Lucy pulled her jacket closed. She'd felt a chill at her back ever since she'd gotten into the car. "It's so cold tonight." Suddenly she was sure something was wrong. Her eyes flicked up to her rear-view mirror.

She scanned the back seat from one side to the other. Nothing. What did she expect to see anyway? She flicked on the interior light. That didn't help to shake her unease.

Where was that copy of *The BFG*? She'd thrown it on the passenger seat but now it was nowhere to be seen. She leaned over and checked the footwell in case it had slid into there. Nothing.

"I...er...bought something for you." Lucy flipped open the glove box. Had she put it in there?

"That's strange... I'm sure I'll find it. Your copy of *The BFG* was in a box I was unpacking and I thought you might like to read it with me again."

Lucy folded up the collar on her coat, wrapping it around her neck. Still the cold pressed at her back, urging her to check the rear-view once more. Instead, she looked up to the house.

Without the book she had nothing to distract her thoughts. Soon she was back where the whispering always led her.

"That night...I didn't worry at first. I gave you an extra half an hour. I just thought you'd gotten carried away playing and had lost track of the time. You were always so good. It was kind of a reward."

The house listened to its grotesque bedtime story.

"I know I should've called Sam's mom straight away. But I didn't think anything was wrong. It's only a block between our houses—such a good, safe, neighborhood. Everyone said so. I'm so sorry, Alex! I should have come to get you. I should have been there!"

The car seemed to grow colder with every word Lucy spoke.

"I wanted to help with the search. I wanted to do something! To look for you, to find you!"

Lucy clenched her hand into a fist, she dug her nails into her palm—part control, part punishment. "I had no idea what he was doing! If I could have been there, I would!"

Just as she did on that terrible night, Lucy looked out into the darkness.

"I waited by the window. Watching, waiting for you. I wanted to be the first person you saw when the police brought you home. I wanted to be there to say, 'It's okay...you're safe, I love you, you're home now.' I waited there all night."

Lucy remembered every terrible second. She'd made herself remember, scored it into her memory. She'd done that to torture herself for not doing more.

"I couldn't pick up the phone when it rang."

Lucy's grief stole her words. She wiped the tears from her face and forced herself to go on.

"When the police did come, you weren't in the car. I couldn't tell you that it was okay, that you were safe...that I love you. I didn't move. I couldn't move, because, if I did, that would be it—that would be giving up, that would be letting go."

She'd stayed at the window while Matt told her what had happened. He'd tried to move her but she'd roughly shaken him off, pushed him away. She couldn't stop looking out. She mustn't stop looking out!

"I'm still looking out now. I'm still waiting, Alex. Haven't I waited long enough? Haven't I?"

Something moved! Just for a moment, in one of the upstairs windows. Something grey, pale—a figure?

"Alex?"

Lucy flung the car door open and ran for the house. Was someone there? Alex? Had he heard her? Swallowed into 1428 Montgomery's huge shadow, she raced across the overgrown lawn. Tangled grass snatched at her ankles, tried to trip her; all the time, Lucy's eyes were fixed on the upstairs window.

She hit the porch and ran to the front door. She pressed herself against it, looking for a way to open it, to get inside. She knew she wasn't strong enough to force it. Instead, she beat on the door, her hammering loud as a scream inside the still house.

"Alex!"

Lucy spotted the mail slot. She knelt down and pushed the metal flap open. She looked into the dark hallway, just as a terrified Jacob had only a few hours before. And, just as Jacob did, she stretched out her fingers and reached inside.

15

Her fingers became her hand, her hand her wrist. Lucy reached deeper through the slot. The sleeve of her coat bunched against the outside of the door, too thick to pass through the gap. On the other side her bare arm stretched into the dark.

It was like reaching into a freezer. With each inch Lucy reached, her arm grew colder, and with each inch the slot gripped her tighter. By the time she'd reached far enough in that she could twist her arm and try for the lock, the rough wood inside the slot was pinching into her skin. Lucy bent her arm, grinding her elbow against the wood, scuffing the skin off the bone. The pain didn't stop her, she just pushed further.

She strained for the lock, her hand feeling a blind path across the back of the door. Her elbow scraped back and forth as she fumbled for the latch. Her blood mixing with Jacob's on the inside of the slot—more offerings to the black house.

She couldn't reach any further. Her fingers strained, scratching against the wood, but she couldn't find the lock. Damn it! She slammed her hand against the inside of the door. She listened to the sound echoing away, her angry clap freed into the darkness of the house. Soon it was swallowed and gone. Still she was locked outside.

With a painful yank, she dislodged her arm from the slot. Her fingers were numb. She massaged them, trying to get the blood flowing again.

"Alex?" Lucy called quietly at the door. "Alex?" She placed a hand against the freezing wood as gently as if she were reaching out to touch the face of the son she thought she'd lost forever.

"Alex." Another emotion crept into Lucy's voice—relief. Could that really have been Alex in the upstairs window? Had he answered her, finally, after all this time?

Lucy closed her eyes. And smiled.

16

L ucy's answering machine had gone. Had she taken Doctor Bachman's advice?

The books, the few ornaments she'd unpacked, the few signs that anyone lived in her apartment, had also gone. Back into their boxes, their lids folded down, not sealed.

T he child's size case weaved through the pedestrians, its worn leather basking in the afternoon sun.

A stop, the sound of a car door being opened, and Lucy loaded the case gently onto the passenger seat. The engine started and she was off.

Late afternoon San Francisco drew across the case, Lucy's journey reflected in the matte leather. Glass and steel reaching for the sky on California, the changing light of a winter afternoon—white to evening gold—flashing in the windows high above.

Eventually the glass gave way to sky. Lucy had broken free of the congested financial district, the sun was stronger, the air clearer, the breath of the sea rushing in from the bay. Lucy picked up speed.

Silhouetted street lamps, one, two, three, raced across the case, Lucy was on the approach to the bridge. Suspension cables took their place cutting through the sky, faster now, flickering like the reflection of a zoetrope.

As Lucy drove, the sun sank lower. It didn't want to be late for its date with the bay, her father used to tell her. When she was a child, they'd lived on the edge of the ocean. Night after night she'd watched the sun sink into the bay. She was six when she asked her father about it. He'd told her that at the end of each day the sun swapped places with the moon, descending to a giant ballroom beneath the sea where it would dance the night away beneath a light show of stars. The moon was much more serious than the sun. Serious but diligent—he'd explained what that meant— and all night long, while the sun danced beneath the sea, the moon would stand guard, watching over the children of the world, keeping them safe until a lazy, happy sun would drift once more into the sky at the start of a new day.

Twenty minutes after they left the bridge, the case arrived at its destination.

Lucy switched off the engine and got out of the car. While she headed around to the trunk. a street lamp blinked on, flickering on the leather of the small case. The trunk was opened and a few moments later slammed shut, then Lucy was at the passenger door. She carefully lifted the case out of the car and, holding it by her side, headed up the path.

It had grown too dark for the case to reflect the world. The crisp afternoon reflections were now muddy and indistinct. A pair of heavy feet in tan brogues shuffled down the path to meet Lucy and her case.

"Hi! Hi! How are you? Great to meet you!"

The man vigorously shook Lucy's hand.

"Well, I've got your keys for you. I just need you to sign these last few documents for me. It's a beautiful house, isn't it? Do you have kids? You have kids? No? Oh well, when the time is right, huh? I'm sure it'll be a wonderful family home!"

The brogues led Lucy and the small case toward the front porch of the house.

"So, you did most of the paperwork with Kelly at the office, that's great! Now, if I can get you to just sign here...and here for me."

Lucy put the case gently down onto the path. The brogues tapped on the ground while Lucy signed.

"And...that...is...it! We're all done! Con-grat-u-lations on your new home! Here are your keys and here's my card. If you need anything—anything at all—just pick up the phone!"

Before he'd even finished his sentence, the estate agent was at his car. He shouted back, "Don't forget, lots of kids! Lots of kids! You'll be very happy! Thanks again! Bye now, bye!"

The ground was wet, a layer of evening dew gathering in the overgrown grass that reached across the path where Lucy had placed the case. In time it would completely overrun the path to 1428 Montgomery.

As the winter sun sank into the bay, Lucy picked up the case and, key in hand, stepped up onto the porch of her new house.

Two days ago, Lucy had beaten on the door that she now stood in front of. Two days ago, she'd made up her mind to find a way to get inside 1428 Montgomery. She could hear from the estate agent's voice (*Lawry*, not Larry) that he couldn't believe his luck when she'd rung. And she could hear that he'd practically fallen off his chair when she'd offered him a figure above the asking price. Her only requirement? That she be in the house as soon as possible. To give *Lawry*, not Larry, his due, he'd turned the whole thing around in thirty-six hours. Everyone wanted rid of the house but Lucy.

Lucy placed a hand against the door.

Are you in there? Are you here?

Lucy slid the key into the lock.

PART TWO

HOPE IS A CORPSE

Hope is a corpse.

A dead thing, watching you suffer with black empty eyes.

Any comfort it might have offered, long since gone to the grave.

1

The smell hit her first, damp and metallic. It pulled itself around the door, growing stronger with every inch Lucy pushed the door open. It filled the hallway. She put a hand up to her face, covering her nose and mouth, as she pressed the door deeper. She realized she wasn't pushing any more, momentum had taken over and the door was moving on its own, a black mouth opening to speak after nine months of silence.

Turn, turn and run! The thought flashed through her mind.

This is insanity!

Lucy hesitated on the porch. What had she done? She turned away, choking on the foul smell that poured from the house. Nine months ago, Alex had been dragged into this place by a monster, and now she was following him.

Nine months ago, Lucy's life had ended. Nine months ago, she'd begun the terrible journey that would lead her to this point. In the darkness, between the words in the articles she hoarded, the whispering had begun. She'd found herself visiting the house every night. She wanted to be with the dead, not the living anymore.

Could Alex really have been calling to her all that time? How could it have taken her so long to hear him?

What had she done? Lucy answered her own question. She'd done what any mother would have done. She took one last breath of dusk air, steeling herself. She stepped over the threshold and the house swallowed her whole.

The sun had not yet fully set outside, but already the hallway was choked with shadows, as if even daylight itself chose not to venture far into the house. Corridors disappeared from the entrance hall, black after the first few feet.

Lucy knew the layout of the house. She'd learned it from the articles she'd read. She knew that through the door to her left was the lounge, to her right a study. Squinting, she could make out the outline of the staircase ahead. She knew what lay up those stairs, what waited for her on the second floor, and it filled her with panic.

She was shaking, the trembling rising through her in waves, each one stronger than the last. The stench grew with every step she took forward. It slithered between her chattering teeth, it filled her mouth, caught in the back of her throat. She spun away from the staircase and rushed for the living room door.

Once he'd been given the all clear by the CSU unit, Detective Bob Taylor had gone from room to room drawing all the curtains, closing off the house from the outside world. What had happened here was unthinkable. It wasn't for reporters and freaks to ogle and rubberneck. He'd never tell Matt and Lucy everything he'd witnessed that night. He'd never be able to forget it either. He was trying to contain the horror. To deny and lock away that terrible blood-soaked room. He couldn't be responsible for it escaping into the world. No one else should ever have to experience what he'd seen.

Before Alex's murder, 1428 Montgomery had been a family home. Ted Lowe, his wife Ann, and their two kids, Todd and Anna, had been on holiday when Alex was snatched. There seemed to be no connection between Alex's kidnapper and the Lowes' house. In the end, the police concluded it was likely sick chance. As simple as Alex's kidnapper seeing the Lowes leaving for their trip alerting him to the house being empty. It was possible he'd passed the house a day later to check there was no one home, but that sighting had been unreliable at best. When he'd returned next, it had been with Alex.

They knew the kidnapper wrapped Alex in a blanket, possibly from the trunk of his car. They'd found fibres caught in what remained of Alex's throat when they'd carried out the autopsy.

Lucy hurried across the lounge, heading for the large bay window. A lone chair, with its high back to her, stood on the far side of the room. Lucy tore the curtains wide. Shadows scattered like startled birds, chased back to the edges of the room by the evening sun.

The fading light wouldn't keep them at bay for long.

Lucy leaned against the window, her breath blasting on the glass, as she fumbled to open the catch. Finally, she threw the window open and stood sucking in the cold evening air, trying to clear her lungs of the dust and the sickening smell, trying to stem the rising panic that was close to overcoming her. No matter what she'd told herself, she wasn't ready for this place.

The Lowes hadn't spent another night in the house after Alex's murder. It had been cleared by a removal firm, each room hastily packed into crates except—if you believed the stories—the room where Alex was murdered.

After what had happened, it would have been understandable if the Lowes had simply abandoned everything in that room, but rumours had spread that Ted Lowe planned to move the contents of what had been his son Todd's room, until Detective Taylor met with him and advised him not to. While Bob Taylor cited extensive damage as the reason for not claiming Todd's belongings, various websites had quoted a leak from the department with a different story: there was just too much blood. The injuries to the bodies from the shotgun blasts had been so severe that bodily matter had been cast over everything the Lowes might have wanted to claim. The leak further claimed that, even before he'd spoken to Ted Lowe, Bob Taylor had arranged with the CTS Decon team to have everything in the room removed and destroyed. Just like drawing the curtains, it was another attempt to protect the world from what he'd seen that night. He couldn't stop the websites from publishing their stories though. And they'd printed far worse in the months leading up to Lucy's collapse.

Lucy stood in the window until she felt strong enough to carry on. Her grip on the frame eased as her nausea passed, and the fresh evening air helped wash the taste of dust and panic from her mouth. Outside the day was dying.

A table had been flipped on its side in the middle of the room and a large ornate mirror hung, dull with dust, reflecting Lucy from the far wall. The shadows had returned, crawling inch by inch across the floorboards, edging closer with each minute the day turned to night.

Lucy left the window and crossed the living room to the door that she knew led into the dining room. Slightly open, it rocked gently on its hinges, back and forth on the breeze from the window she'd opened. As she left the living room a thought, quiet, like a barely audible voice, entered her mind: she would never leave this place again.

2

Each room was the same, half packed as if the removal company had abandoned their work without warning. The chair that faced the wall in the living room, the overturned table, a stack of books in the corner of the dining room, all left behind to rot in the dark. Lucy stepped over an ivy, its pot on its side, a trail of brittle vines reaching out toward the curtained window. Withered limbs trying to make it to the light before they died.

The track caught Lucy's eye because it was darker than the rest of the kitchen floor. Cutting through the dust, a thin path weaved across the boards and wound into the wall where it stopped. Lucy traced the trail back from the wall, past her and into the dining room she'd just left. A rat maybe? Had *Lawry*, not Larry, moved something ahead of her arrival? There weren't any footprints in the dust. If there were rats, it might go some way to explaining the smell.

The boy's face stopped Lucy in her tracks. Smiling from behind the shattered glass, she felt his gaze as sure as if he were in the study with her. The photograph must have fallen from Ted Lowe's desk when the house was being cleared. It had lodged behind the pipes that fed the radiator. The Lowes must have noticed that the photograph was missing. That hadn't been enough to draw them back to this place to look for it.

Lucy knelt down and eased the frame out from behind the pipes. The broken pieces of glass shifted and ground against one another as she lifted the photograph. Gently, she placed it face down on the floor of the study. She couldn't bear to look at Todd Lowe's smiling face. His happiness made the insatiable emptiness of her grief claw inside her. There was nothing of her left, but still it hungered for more.

Room by room, Lucy moved through the ground floor. In truth, she was delaying the inevitable. Too soon she found herself back in the entrance hall with the staircase stretching ahead of her. She wasn't ready for this. She couldn't face this.

"Alex?" she called up the stairs. *Please answer me. Don't make me do this.*

Silence. Lucy wrapped a hand around the bannister and dragged herself onto the bottom stair. Her nausea had returned, her throat was clogged with dust. She couldn't breathe. Everything had been leading her to this point. She'd seen the figure in the upstairs window, grey against the glass. Upstairs where the monster had dragged her son. Upstairs to the second room along the corridor...

"Alex!" *Please answer me! Please!*

Lucy climbed onto the second stair.

The phone call had come from a concerned neighbor. Elsa Tan had been woken by what she thought was a gunshot from Ted Lowe's place. It could have just been a car backfiring but she thought it best to ring it in, "what with the Lowes being away and all".

Initially, a patrol car had been despatched to check the house. When they found the front door ajar, Officer Hernandez and his partner had made their way inside.

Two days after Alex had been found, Bob Taylor sat down with Officer Hernandez and his partner, Officer Abigail Redmond. Neither looked like they'd slept since that night. Redmond cried quietly through the fifteen-minute conversation; and Hernandez was distant, unable to make eye contact. Hernandez and Redmond had given their statements in the hours after they'd discovered Alex. Bob Taylor had tried to make sure they were processed and allowed off duty as quickly as possible. He spoke to their sergeant and they were both placed on leave, pending interviews with a department counsellor. When Bob Taylor had last seen Redmond, she'd been covered in Alex's blood.

Before driving to the meeting, Bob Taylor moved from room to room drawing the curtains across all of 1428 Montgomery's windows. In meeting with Hernandez and Redmond, he was attempting to do the same thing. He asked them, as a favour to him, to never speak of what they'd seen in that room. They couldn't save Alex, he couldn't protect them from what they had been through—but they could protect a mother and father who had lost their son. If they ever found out what had really happened ... How could any parent survive that?

Step by step, Lucy pulled herself up the staircase, up to the second floor and the nightmares that waited for her.

3

For almost two months Bob Taylor managed to keep the full details of Alex's death from the public.

Officer Hernandez quit the force three weeks after the murders. He confessed to the department counsellor that he'd thought about killing himself. He couldn't stop reliving what he'd seen. Every night, the faceless boy was waiting for him in the dark.

"If there was a God he'd have killed that kid straight away! How could he have kept him alive...like that?"

A month after that meeting, Karen Guzman had followed Lucas Hernandez to the bar where he now spent most of his days. She'd kept the drinks flowing until he could barely lift his head. Then she'd convinced him that the only way to stop the broken boy from visiting him each night was to tell her his story. Share his burden. He'd told her everything. He had no idea that she worked for *The Post*. The next morning the whole world knew all the terrible details that Bob Taylor had fought to keep from them.

Hernandez and Redmond had found the front door to 1428 Montgomery half open. Broken glass had been cast across the hallway floor. A trail of stars, flickering in the beam of Redmond's torch as she traced it back to one of the stained-glass panes that framed the door. Alex's kidnapper had smashed it, reached in through the jagged opening and unlocked the door from the inside. The Officers were at the foot of the stairs when Hernandez signalled for Redmond to stop.

"Can you hear that?" The sound of their movement settled. Redmond had only been on the job for eight months. She leaned into the darkness, eager, alert, trying to pull any sound out of the black. The breathing made her start.

Wet, gurgling, it came fast and desperate. It filled her with such immediate horror that she flung out a hand and grabbed Hernandez's arm. The sound came again. Wheezing, choking.

"Oh my God, what is that?"

Hernandez couldn't answer her. He'd frozen, his radio inches from his mouth. Any chance he might call for backup stolen by the fear that had seized him. The third time the sound burst from the night, it was a scream.

Mewling and terrible, like a dying animal, the broken boy cried out—a long, pitiful wail full of pain and fear. Gripping Hernandez's arm tighter than ever, Redmond began to climb the stairs. Alex screamed again. She pulled herself forward, her mind squirming with awful flashes of what might lay writhing in the darkness ahead.

"Oh Christ! What is that? Red, what—"

Another scream cut Hernandez's rambling short. They had reached the top of the stairs.

Deeper, darker, further away from the outside world, Lucy reached the second floor. A heavy oak wardrobe stood abandoned at the top of the stairs. Its large door rested ajar, the outline of the mirror it once held burnt into its varnish by years of sunlight. Lucy's eyes were drawn to the wardrobe's black innards as she passed it.

Lucy wrapped her hands together, trying to keep her trembling under control. She might only be a few feet from the answers she sought but she wasn't sure her body could carry her that far.

"Alex?" Her voice was rough, small, calling down the corridor, one ghost searching for another.

In the article Karen Guzman had written after she'd tricked Hernandez, she'd described this corridor with as much lurid detail as she'd afforded every terrible moment of Alex's death. Guzman had taken her time, describing Hernandez and Redmond's fearful approach, their *twenty steps to the slaughterhouse*, relishing building the atmosphere before the main event. Matt blamed that article for pushing Lucy over the edge.

Because of Guzman, Lucy knew that through the ivory painted door to her left was Ted and Ann Lowe's bedroom. A large bed still stood in the middle of the room. A white dust sheet thrown over it, it looked more like a tomb in a crypt than a bed in a family home.

Lucy felt a tear streak her cheek. She'd tried so hard to be strong, dragged herself to this point, but she had nothing left. *Please don't make me do this!* The corridor wrapped tightly around her. With every step it seemed to grow smaller.

Ahead on the right was the second bedroom. Because of Guzman, Lucy knew that Ted and Ann Lowe had recorded Todd's height on the wall next to the door. The lines were where she expected them to be. A new one for each birthday... *4, 5, 6...* Ted had written *LITTLE MAN! BIG MAN! GIANT!* next to his son's annual measurements. Lucy gritted her teeth, grinding them, trying to hold herself together. Because of Guzman, she knew that beyond that door was the room where her life had ended.

4

She couldn't do it. After everything, she couldn't open the door. Even though she knew now, was sure now, that it was in the window of this room she'd seen the grey figure. Pale skin glimpsed just for a moment. Could he really be here?

"Alex?" Lucy called weakly at the door.

Don't make me do this.

"Alex?" She closed her eyes. Hernandez's words were waiting for her in the black. *If there was a God he'd have killed that kid straight away! How could he have kept him alive...like that?*

Lucy's fingers closed around the handle and she turned it.

For nine months the house had whispered; now it screamed. Lucy opened her eyes. She'd read all the articles, hoarded all the words, she knew every detail that Bob Taylor had tried so hard to protect her from, but finally stepping into the room where Alex died crushed her.

On the far wall, someone had attempted to repair the damage from the gun shot that killed Alex. A large patch of plaster, at what would have been the height of Alex's head, had been roughly smeared onto the wall. A sob, pure grief torn from her heart, burst from Lucy's lips.

She knew the shot had thrown Alex backwards, his tiny body slammed into the wall. Gloss paint had been rolled across the raw plaster, a high shine on an otherwise matte wall. The colours didn't even match. Lucy staggered across the room, her legs close to giving out beneath her. She stopped in front of the botched repair. Now she was standing over the place where Alex had died. She reached out and touched the rough plaster. Mould had spread through the gloss paint, the truth refusing to be silenced. It had taken forty-five minutes for Alex to die. Redmond had sat with him for over thirty of those minutes. She'd cradled what was left of his skull in her lap, trying desperately to find a way to stem his suffering. Lucy fell to her knees in front of the wall and sobbed.

Alex had screamed, that awful broken scream, until the paramedics had arrived. They knew they couldn't move him but they couldn't treat him either. His wounds were so severe he should have been dead already. Redmond had begged the paramedics to do something. All they could do was inject him with morphine for the pain. He screamed for another fifteen minutes until he finally fell silent. Bob Taylor had arrived at the same time as the paramedics. Once he realized there was nothing that could be done, he'd ordered the room be cleared and had sat with Redmond, Hernandez and Alex. He'd held Alex's hand and prayed for the end to come quickly.

How could she not have been there? *What sort of mother lets her son die terrified and in agony, surrounded by strangers? Where were you when he needed you? When he screamed for you?* Lucy gritted her teeth. *Stop crying!* She wouldn't let the pain out. She didn't deserve to let the pain out. She had to keep her grief inside, inside where it dug and scraped, where it tore and gouged her, every day until her dead heart finally stopped beating. She'd failed him completely and this was her sentence. In her eyes, no amount of pain or suffering could ever make amends for what she'd done.

Alex wasn't the only person to die in Todd Lowe's room that night. Behind Lucy, on the wall by the door, a second patch of raw plaster indicated all too clearly where Alex's murderer had ended his life. Whoever had carried out the repairs to this room hadn't even bothered to paint over the second patch.

In Guzman's article, she'd described in vivid detail how Alex's screams had driven his murderer to put the shotgun in his own mouth. How looking down through the mist of blood that hung in the air, seeing that ripped-apart face looking up at him, possessed him with such guilt that he put the burning hot barrel between his teeth. His hand—slippery with Alex's blood—found the trigger. The blast emptied his skull, his face collapsing, flames and blood where his eyes should have been. His suffering had ended in an instant.

Lucy wished he'd hesitated, that he hadn't been able to go through with it. He should have been made to witness every single moment Alex suffered, to listen to every terrible scream. He should have survived that night so that she could see him, confront him. Every fibre of her wanted to rip and tear at his flesh, to pummel and break him. To crush him. She wanted to hear him scream, to cry out, to beg for his worthless life. Then she wanted to beat him to death with the hands he'd left empty—

Lucy couldn't breathe. She could see it all. The air was thick with blood, she could taste the metal in her mouth. There was so much blood! She stumbled for the window.

She grabbed at the catch and twisted it open. The window wouldn't budge! It had been painted shut. She tried the smaller one above it, and the one next to it. They'd all been painted shut. Lucy collapsed against the pane. She pressed her face against the cold glass and wept. What had she expected? What had she imagined would happen?

"Oh, Alex! Where are you?"

Then Lucy noticed the curtains.

Bob Taylor had gone from room to room drawing closed all the curtains—she knew that from Guzman's article. There was no way he would have forgotten the most important room in the house. Lucy stood up. Someone had opened the curtains. Maybe just enough that they would be seen. The grey figure she'd glimpsed two nights ago? She realized she was standing where that figure had stood. Alex? *Please let it be true.*

Glen was late. He should have been home half an hour ago. His feet pumped the pedals on his bike. Come on! Mom was going to freak out! She'd lose her shit for sure! Rod always said that and it always made him smile. How would she do that exactly? Where would she lose it? Of all the things she was going to lose—

Glen saw the shapes and slammed his feet down on the path. His shoes skidded along the ground. He dug his heels in and jerked to a stop. Who was that? Who were the two figures standing in the window of *that* room?

Lucy saw Glen stop. She watched him watching her. She knew now what she had to do. Wiping her tears, she turned back to face the awful room behind her.

Glen watched Lucy leave the window. The second figure remained.

5

Lucy sat at the kitchen table with her back to the open door. In the hour that had passed since she stood in the window, the darkness in the house had swelled until it massed in every room.

So many places to hide.

Lucy hadn't arranged for the power to be switched on. That could wait. She only cared about getting into the house. She only cared about getting to Alex.

She'd found a box of candles in one of the kitchen drawers. Now their light formed a flickering last stand against the night.

Lucy listened to the living room door knocking gently on its hinges. She listened, silent and focussed, to every sound the house made. Most of all she listened for any noise from Todd Lowe's room. Above her, the ceiling was mottled, freckles of mould spreading across the white paint. More decay. An ornate ceiling rose circled a redundant light fitting. Its shadow jittered, stretching and shrinking in the candle light. Someone had removed the bulb from the socket. Lucy thought that was odd considering how much had been left behind when the Lowes had moved. Her eyes returned to her hands resting on the small suitcase in front of her.

Twice in the last hour she'd moved her fingers to its catches, and twice she returned them to rest on top. The worn leather was warm, as if it had a heat of its own, a life radiating from within. It had been in her family for years. She'd taken it with her on every trip she'd made as a child. Each night before she'd left for camp, or one of her "expeditions", as her father had called them, they'd packed the case together. When they were done, he'd attempt to lift the case. He'd puff and groan, feigning that he couldn't lift the huge weight they'd crammed inside. He'd shake his head.

"Too many biscuits!" he'd frown.

"But we didn't pack any biscuits!" Lucy would protest, laughing as he pretended to struggle and strain.

Then, on her first night away, when she missed home the most, she'd open her case and there on top of her clothes would be two packets of her favorite biscuits. She never knew how her father managed to smuggle them into her packing. She was eight and it seemed like magic to her. That was a lifetime ago. Lucy knew what waited inside the case tonight. She'd packed it herself, the night she left Matt. She was glad her father had died long before any of this had happened.

She reached again for the catches and, for the first time in seven months, flicked them open.

Two months after Alex died, Matt had suggested they move some of his things into storage. Lucy had known what that meant. Once they'd begun to dismantle Alex's room, they would never be able to put it back together again. Once his toys, his clothes, his memory, had been shifted into a dark storage container somewhere, they would never return. She couldn't let that happen. Matt had tried to persuade her it would help them heal. That was the same day he found her cuttings. That night she packed Alex's case and left.

With trembling hands, Lucy touched the soft material of the red sweater. It had been Alex's favorite. The warmest one, the softest one. He'd picked it out himself. It had been far too big for him when they'd bought it. By the end, it had just about fitted him. Lucy sighed. She lifted the sweater carefully from the case and breathed deeply the smell of him. His wonderful smell! For seven months she'd dreamed of breathing that scent once more. The smell of his hair, Sunday nights, when she'd bath him, and afterwards they'd sit in the high-backed chair in the lounge, watching cartoons until he fell asleep in her arms. For seven months she'd ached to open his case. But she'd always stopped herself, knowing that once she'd sprung the catches and lifted the lid, his smell would begin to fade. But now was the time, now she hoped the smell of his clothes, the toys and books that she had packed in the case, would call to him, draw him through the darkness to her once more. She closed her eyes. In her mind she saw him running, feet drumming across the varnished boards of their old house—a blur of red, laughing, racing away—and then he was gone. She tried to hold onto the memory, tried to fix it in her mind, but all she could see was the rough plaster smeared onto the wall in that terrible room.

Lucy looked up to the ceiling once more. As she did, one of the candles flared and burned out, its wick collapsing with a hiss, consumed into the hot wax it had created. The darkness that waited patiently in the doorway behind her edged a little closer. The remaining candles would last another hour at most.

"Alex. Alex. I'm here now."

Lucy listened.

"It's okay. I'm here now." She could no longer hear the lounge door knocking.

"Alex, if you can talk to me, please say something."

She kept her eyes on the ceiling as she spoke, straining to hear even the slightest sound—a movement on the stairs, a board shifting under the weight of a foot in Todd Lowe's room—anything to confirm she'd been heard.

"Was it you I saw at the window? It was, wasn't it?" Lucy spoke quietly, gently. "It's okay. Mommy's here now. Mommy's here now."

6

Early morning sun, amber through the dirty window, bled into the kitchen. The candles had long since died, melted to pools, wax stalactites spilling from the counter tops where they'd stood. The last candle had flared and sputtered out just over an hour after Lucy opened Alex's case. She hadn't flinched when the thick darkness had washed over her, consuming the room in an instant. She'd simply waited in front of the open case, whispering into the night and listening for any sound in return, hoping the grey-skinned figure she'd glimpsed in the window would try to find her in the black.

But the darkness had brought with it only silence.

Hour upon hour of it.

Eventually, the sun had begun to rise and the darkness had retreated to the kitchen doorway once more. Lucy's shadow stretched after it. She hadn't finished with the night yet. Silent and still, Lucy waited at the kitchen table. She would wait for as long as it took to hear from Alex. When he was ready she would be here.

Hers wasn't the only shadow to reach across the kitchen tiles. All around Lucy, black fingers snaked from the doorway. The shadow of the chair, the table, the corrupted remains of the candles; and one more. One long black shape that hid among the others, inconspicuous at first. Until it began to move.

A slow shift, and then fast, towards Lucy.

Suddenly someone was knocking on the kitchen window.

"Hello? Hello? Is someone there?" The figure leaned against the window trying to look inside.

She recognized the voice straight away.

"Hello?" Matt called again.

Lucy got up quick, almost throwing her chair over. She backed up, away from the window, out through the kitchen door and into the hallway. Had he seen her? Matt's shadow swept across the kitchen floor and disappeared.

Lucy crossed the dim entrance hall, clinging to the shadows on the edge of the room. She thought about running upstairs, maybe running from the house. No, she couldn't leave Alex now—

Matt's silhouette loomed up to the stained-glass panes surrounding the front door. The movement made Lucy jump. She ducked back against the wall.

"Hello? Look, I'm sorry to bother you. It's just… It's my wife. She… she's not very well. Her car's been parked outside your house since last night. I'm worried something might have happened to her. Have you seen her? Please."

Lucy leaned against the cold wall. Matt's concern made tears well in her eyes. For a moment she thought he might understand. She wanted him to understand.

No. No, he wouldn't.

"I can't help you." Lucy's voice was rough, the emotion barely hidden. She pressed against the wall, waiting for Matt to leave.

"Lucy? Is that you?"

He knows! What now?

"Lucy! Open the door!" Matt leaned into the glass. "Lucy!"

After a long moment Lucy opened the door. She held her foot against it so it couldn't be opened any further than she wanted.

"Lucy? What's going on?" Matt looked at Lucy and his heart sank. She looked terrible, exhausted, her eyes were wild and distant. He'd seen her like this before, in the weeks leading up to her hospitalization. The Lucy he loved coming apart at the seams.

"Are you okay? How did you get in there? Did you break in? Come on, we've got to get you out of here before someone sees." He reached for her arm.

"No. No!" Lucy pulled away.

"What's going on?"

"I didn't break in, Matt. You should go."

"What do you mean? What have you done, Lucy?"

"What have I done? Don't look at me like that! I did what had to be done. What? Was I going to wait for you to do something? You left him here! You left him here alone for six months while I was rotting in that hospital!"

"Left him here? Lucy, Alex isn't here."

"That's what I thought too! But I've seen him. Oh, Matt, I've seen him!"

"That's not possible."

"You're wrong. I've seen him and I'm going to find him. I'm going to find him and I'm going to make sure he's okay."

"He's dead, Lucy! He's dead," Matt snapped, his pain and frustration boiling over. "He isn't anywhere any more. For God's sake, listen to yourself! You can't bring him back from the dead!"

Lucy gripped the door with white knuckles. She was crying, but it was anger that had brought her to tears. She was furious, close to slamming the door in Matt's face. "I knew you wouldn't understand! You wanted to burn this place down. Don't try and deny it! You told me! You wanted to burn this house to the ground, with him in it!"

Matt felt sick. In the months after Alex's murder, he'd watched, helpless, as Lucy slowly went out of her mind. It had been terrible, but in all that time, through those grinding, bleak months she'd never spoken like this, she'd never lost track of reality. He understood her hoarding of cuttings, her need for answers, her obsessive poring over every detail of Alex's murder. But every one of her obsessions had ended at the same point, at the same crushing conclusion: that every beautiful thing their boy had been, or would ever be, had ended on that awful April night. Listening to her now, he felt a new, somehow even more dreadful, sadness wrap around his heart.

"Lucy, there's nothing for you here. Please let me help you."

Lucy fell silent. Somewhere, deep inside, a part of her knew she might be out of control, that she should listen to Matt, get help, get out of the house before it was too late. But that part didn't stand a chance while the deafening whisper of 1428 Montgomery promised her that she might see her son again.

"I don't need anyone's help. I just need Alex."

Lucy closed the door on Matt. She locked it and stepped away. She walked to the bottom of the stairs and looked up. Up to where the shadows swirled, safe, away from the prying eyes of the early morning sun.

"Alex, please."

Lucy stood before the darkness, willing Alex to appear, to give her a sign, anything to end the months of torture.

Nothing.

Lucy was utterly alone.

7

And she remained alone, living in that hopeless place, the ghost of 1428 Montgomery. At night, if you pressed your ear to the freezing front door, you might hear her sobbing in the upstairs room where Alex died.

8

Plates piled in the kitchen sink, the remains of the little Lucy did eat unwashed and discarded. Takeaway cartons, abandoned for the flies, littered the bench tops. After Matt left, she'd moved from room to room redrawing any of the curtains she'd disturbed. She knew now that if Alex were to appear to her, it would be in the darkness, so she set about blocking out any light that might scare him away.

A single candle burned low, frail against the night. Alex's case had gone from the kitchen table. It had been replaced with an overflowing ashtray and a collection of thumbed books on the occult. *The Dead Are Around Us*—its spine broken so its pages would lay open where Lucy had been reading. She'd scribbled angry notes in the margins of another text, *Speaking With The Dead*, and a copy of *They Are Not Gone* lay open at an illustration of a Victorian woman sat at a table performing a séance with a Ouija board. In the image, pale faces pulled from the sketched shadows that whirled around her. One smiled, another screamed, a third was horribly contorted, as if possessed by a terrible madness: the faces of the dead, waiting in the dark for the living to bring them forth

Lucy's chair was empty, twisted away from the table as if she'd gotten up in a hurry. It had come to rest facing the open door to the hallway, looking into the deep black that lay beyond. Suddenly a scream, the sound of metal grinding on metal, roared through the kitchen. The waste disposal spun up with a metallic howl. At the same time lights began to blink on: in the study, the lounge, upstairs in Ted and Ann Lowe's bedroom... The power had been switched back on.

No lights blinked on in the hall. In fact, the darkness seemed to press forward, deeper into the kitchen doorway as if it had been waiting for the thundering noise to cover its approach. Just beyond the door something shifted in the black.

"For God's sake!" Lucy shouted. She burst into the kitchen, heading for the sink. She slammed her hand on the switch, shutting off the waste disposal. The grinding wound down and stopped.

Lucy leaned against the bench, the metal scream still ringing in her ears. The noise had startled her, yes, but for a moment, she'd thought something was finally happening. The vacuum that replaced the screeching was a crushing blow, the same hopeless silence that had filled the house since she'd arrived. She was pale, exhausted; she'd started drinking early today.

In the hallway, Alex laughed.

Lucy pushed herself off from the bench. She was walking in thick mud, booze and exhaustion catching at her heels as she stepped sluggishly for the hall. Alex laughed again.

Lucy loved that laugh, it had brought her such joy when Alex had been alive. Now all it brought her was pain. The power coming on must have triggered her answering machine.

"Shut up! Just shut up!"

Clumsily, she hammered for the machine's off switch. She stopped the playback but didn't notice she'd hit the record button at the same time. A red light blinked on indicating the machine was listening.

Lucy pulled herself back up the stairs. As she neared the top, the hulking shape of the wardrobe came into view. Was its door open wider than when she'd passed it before? She slapped her hand down on the landing light switch and plunged the upstairs hallway back into darkness. She headed along the corridor flicking off each light she came to. Room by room, the night reclaimed the house.

The candle in Todd Lowe's room cast a dim glow over the bare boards and up onto the bare wall behind it. Less than a year before, Todd's room had buzzed with the endless energy of a smart six-year-old boy. It'd been a safe haven. A place where the rough edges of the world were dulled to soft pillows and warm pyjamas. Dinosaurs warred aliens nightly on the windowsill. Todd had chosen his own wallpaper: space, specked with stars, where cartoon galaxies swirled across the walls and rocket ships sped towards the most dangerous and mysterious unexplored planets, the ones closest to the ceiling, in the corner where Todd Lowe's bed had stood. After the murder, when the CTS Decon team had cleared the room, they'd had to strip that wallpaper too. Now, all that remained of Tod Lowe's dreams were a few scraps of torn paper in the high corners of the room. As the dim circle of light trembled on the bare boards and the bare wall, it was hard to imagine anyone had ever found comfort in this stripped and sanitized room.

A small figure stood on the edge of the candlelight, its face masked in the shadows. Lucy had unpacked a few of Alex's toys and books, she'd placed them in a rough circle around his case. *The Wizard of Earthsea*, a *Spiderman* comic, his homework book, *Optimus Prime*, and his favorite, the toy she hoped he'd be drawn to the most, an *Action Jack* figure, closest to the case and closest to her.

Lucy leaned against the wall to steady herself as she crossed the room. She sat heavily down on the floor in front of Alex's case. Her movement set the candle's flame swaying, and for a moment, Action Jack was swallowed into the shadows altogether. Darkness had followed Lucy into the circle.

After Matt's visit she'd decided to move into Todd Lowe's room, deeper into the house, away from prying eyes and interference. That was where she'd seen him, the shape in the window, and that would be where she would see Alex again. She was sure of that.

She'd bought a Ouija board the morning after she'd seen the figure in the window. Before that day she'd had no idea how easy it was to buy one. There was a whole shelf of them, in the board games section, propped up between *Monopoly* and *Scrabble*.

Lawry, not Larry, had returned her call when she'd been coming out of the store. The ringing of her cell phone had startled her, not because she wasn't expecting him, but because, when she looked around, looked down at the shopping bag in her hands, she couldn't remember how she'd gotten to the mall. She didn't remember leaving her apartment, or the drive. She had no idea where she'd parked her car. She felt like she'd been sleepwalking and Lawry's call had woken her. It wasn't the first time she'd lost minutes, even hours. She'd blacked out whole days with booze and pills. She had to, it was the only way to survive. But she hadn't been drinking that morning. She put a hand to her other ear, to block out the noise around her, to try to focus on Lawry's words. Even then, the sound of the whispering was so loud she could barely hear her own thoughts.

She'd neatly folded Alex's sweater and placed it on top of his case. As the sun sank into the bay on that second evening, she'd unfolded the Ouija board on that precious red material. That night she'd talked to him again, calling into the dark, her hands resting lightly on the Ouija board's planchette, desperate for a sign that he heard her. None had come. Hour after hour the empty silence had worn her down. She'd whispered until her voice was hoarse, until her calls became pleas, until she begged for him to answer her.

Two more nights of silence had followed.

Lucy refilled her glass. She'd gotten a taste for whiskey living with Matt. He wouldn't drink anything else. He wouldn't have drunk this. It tasted as bad as it smelled. She took a large mouthful. And then another.

She rested her fingers softly on the planchette. She closed her eyes and sighed. She couldn't take much more of this.

"I'm sorry, Alex. I didn't mean what I said downstairs. I don't want you to shut up. I don't want that at all. I'm...I'm just tired and it hurts."

The candle's flame had slowed. Action Jack's face slipped in and out of the shadows.

"Please, Alex."

All around her, darkness pressed on the edges of the candle's glow. Like the woman in the illustration, she was surrounded by the shifting night.

"Can you hear me? Can you move the pointer?"

Lucy opened her eyes. Was someone watching her? She looked past the candle's glow, over towards the window where she'd seen the grey figure.

"Alex, are you here?"

The planchette remained motionless.

"Is it the light? It's too light, isn't it?"

She snatched forward and snuffed the candle. Hot wax stung her fingertips. The night snapped closed around her.

Lucy leaned forward, into the darkness, waiting for her eyes to adjust. The glow from the candle's flame had left a red smudge on her retina, it followed her gaze as her eyes swept around the room. She felt the hairs lifting on the back of her neck. The cold seemed to have drawn closer the moment the candle had gone out.

Lucy stretched a hand through the frigid air. She found the edge of the case and walked her fingers across it until they rested gently on the planchette once more.

"Alex, I saw you in the window, didn't I? I know you were here."

The case developed from the gloom ahead, "Please, are you here now?"

The room grew around her as her eyes adjusted. The Ouija board, the case, her hands reaching into the black. She longed for the grey skin to draw out of the shadows towards her.

"I love you son, please say something, talk to me."

The planchette remained motionless.

"Why won't you talk to me? Alex? How many nights do you want me to wait? What have I done?"

Lucy took another drink. And then another. The silence was desolate, utterly empty. Alex wasn't here. Perhaps he hadn't ever been. She started to cry. She could taste her tears, salty on her lips as she drained her glass. She fumbled for the bottle; it rocked back, almost toppling, as she found its neck in the dark. She filled the glass until she felt whiskey pouring over her fingers. This would be the fourth night of silence.

"Alex, please! I need to know if you're here. Please, make a noise, a sound…"

Nothing.

"I just want to talk to you one more time. You can't be gone! Please. You can't! I love you so much!"

Lucy searched the darkness, desperate for even the smallest sign that she'd been heard. But, as her eyes grew more accustomed to the dark, the only thing to appear was the wall ahead and the rough plaster plug callously marking where a shotgun blast had torn through her boy. Lucy screamed, her grief igniting into rage. She hurled her glass against the wall. It exploded against the mould riddled plaster.

"FUCK YOU! FUCK YOU! YOU HEAR ME?" Lucy climbed to her feet. Whiskey ran down the wall, black streaks where Alex's blood had poured nine months before. "You took my son! Why? Why?" Lucy screamed at the ceiling. "What did I ever do? What did he do to deserve this? You fucking monster! What did you do? What did you do?"

Lucy stood, defiantly demanding an answer. Tears of fury spilled over her cheeks but she would not back down.

She hadn't noticed but the planchette on the Ouija board had moved. It had come to rest highlighting a single word: NO.

9

Lucy stirred. She was lying on the floor. She didn't know how she got there.

Winter sunlight streamed in through the open curtains. Her head throbbed. She closed her eyes again but that didn't help. The world glowed red and angry against her eyelids. Slowly, she rolled onto her side. The smell of whiskey sent a wave of nausea welling up from her stomach into her throat. Last night's bottle lay empty beside her. She pushed it away, trying to breathe through the sickness. It rattled lazily across the stripped boards, coming to a stop against the wall with a hollow clunk.

Lucy brought her arm up to her face so she could read her watch. It was just past 4:00pm. She'd slept through the whole day. In a little over an hour it would be dark again. The Ouija board lay face down, knocked onto the floor. She didn't remember doing that either.

Gently, she hauled herself up into a sitting position. She planted her hands on the floor, as if that might somehow anchor the room that was swaying around her.

The bedroom door was closed. She didn't remember shutting herself in. What she did remember of last night came in flashes, scattered black pieces. She shivered. Was it the cold that had woken her? She hazily remembered the temperature dropping, freezing air wrapping itself around her, drawing the warmth from her body—and then the light was there, burning her eyes.

Something was wrong. Lucy turned to look behind her.

10

A small cry escaped her lips. She clapped a hand over her mouth and scuttled back away from the wall.

Scrawled across the wall in large, malformed letters was a message:

DON'T LET THEM CATCH YOU LOOKING

Lucy's eyes darted around the room.

What's going on?

"Alex?" Her quiet words were startling against the stillness of the house.

"Alex, did you do this?"

Don't let them catch you looking.

Don't let *who* catch you looking?

The house remained silent. But it was no longer the empty silence that had filled the house every day since Lucy had moved in. Something had changed. The soundless room felt charged, filled with electricity. It felt like it was waiting.

Listening.

Lucy could hear her blood rushing in her ears. "Alex?"

She edged across the room towards the message. When she saw the chips of plaster beneath the letters she stopped.

The words hadn't been written on the wall, they'd been *carved* into it.

It's a warning.

But...from Alex?

Had she finally contacted him?

That thought alone was enough to pull her forward once more. Onwards until she found herself sitting in front of the words. She reached out a trembling hand and touched the letters. Plaster dust painted her fingertips, broken pieces caught and bit at her skin. She ran her fingers over the letters, feeling in the cracks and grooves as if she were searching for an answer, a connection, something only a mother could find. Had her boy been here? Was this the sign she'd longed for? Outside, the afternoon sun was quickly changing from white to orange, day into winter dusk.

Lucy hauled herself to her feet. She backed away, across the room to the bedroom door. She couldn't take her eyes off the message. If she'd contacted Alex, why would he have written this?

Reaching behind her, Lucy felt along the door until she found the handle. She turned it. She felt the door shift as the latch pulled back.

Something slammed into the door from the other side.

Lucy screamed and wheeled around.

The door knocked gently in its frame. What was happening? Was someone on the other side? Impulsively, Lucy stuck out a foot, planting it behind the door to stop it from opening any further. Would that really stop anyone if they barged against the other side? It had stopped the knocking. The house fell silent once more.

She leaned in towards the door, listening for any movement in the corridor beyond. It was hard to hear anything over her own fast, scared breathing. She took the handle in her hand.

She slipped her foot back.

And tore the door open.

For a long moment she stood behind it, ready to use it as a shield should anything tear out of the dim corridor towards her.

Eventually she got up the nerve to lean out of the room. The dim light from the window behind her didn't stretch far along the corridor. Lucy followed the wall with her eyes. The hallway seemed empty, but the hulking frame of the open wardrobe blocked her view before she could see to the stairs.

Soon, even the light at her back would be gone and the night would crawl from its daytime hiding place once more. Lucy turned back to the message cut into the wall, and then to her Ouija board.

11

Huddled at the end of the corridor, peeking around the wardrobe, the darkness watched Lucy turn to look behind her. It watched her head back into the room and, after a time, it followed her.

Night was closing in fast now. Lucy gathered up the Ouija board and its planchette. She didn't bother to light a candle. She was only interested in one thing: contacting Alex.

She set up the Ouija on the floor close to the wall. In the fading light she reached a hand up to the message. She ran her fingers over the broken letters. **DON'T LET THEM CATCH YOU LOOKING**. Lucy rested her other hand on the Ouija board's planchette.

"Alex, I know you're here." She looked around the room. It seemed to be shrinking around her, the last grey evening light corralled into the middle of the room.

"Please, son, talk to me."

She willed the planchette to move beneath her fingertips.

It remained still.

"It's okay, Mommy's here."

The thick darkness of the hallway had reached the open doorway behind Lucy.

"Can you move the pointer? Can you show me that you're here?"

Beyond the doorway the corridor was pitch, disorienting black that stretched past the open door to Ted and Ann Lowe's bedroom and on to the ajar wardrobe at the top of the stairs. Whatever had carved the words into the wall of Todd's room while Lucy lay unconscious, this was its domain: the darkness of a nightmare, drenched in sweat and panic, a fever dream where black limbs spilled, twisted and wet, onto the stripped wooden floor. An unspeakable darkness, where grasping fingers, caked in putrescence, shot out and snapped tight around white flesh.

A shrill scream in the entrance hall: the phone began to ring. It cried out in the dark until Lucy's answering machine kicked in. Alex laughed and the familiar message began to play: "Hi! You're through to the Campbell Clan. I'm afraid..." The message cut out.

The hallway fell silent once more.

Then, something shifted close by the machine. Seconds later it was on the stairs, dragging itself up through the darkness: the ghost of Lucy Campbell pulling herself up to the second floor. Recorded over her message last night when she'd drunkenly tried to turn off the answering machine, the sound of her footsteps faded, moving out of range of the cheap microphone, and once more the hallway fell quiet.

Next, static, a scratch of interference on the recording, was followed by something else: movement. It wasn't Lucy this time, she'd returned to her vigil in Todd Lowe's room. The movement came again, closer, something dragging itself across the hallway floor. Sliding, squelching, it pulled its raw form towards the machine. But then, far worse than any shape the recording evoked, came a voice. Two words, barked, rough and distorted: "NO GOD".

The recording cut out.

The machine beeped.

Another voice began to speak.

"Hello? Lucy? Is someone there? Lucy, it's Doctor Bachman. Matt called me. He told me... I...er...I didn't believe it at first. Lucy, please listen to me. You shouldn't stay a moment longer in that place."

The black house fed on Doctor Bachman's words, drinking in his concern.

"It's very bad for you, Lucy. Look, here's my home number. Please call me. If I don't hear from you tonight I'm going to come to the house tomorrow to talk with you. Please Lucy, leave tonight. Call me and let me know you've gone."

Doctor Bachman repeated his number twice. He waited on the line until the machine cut him off. Any last rays of evening light that had ventured into the house had now been smothered. Throughout 1428 Montgomery the darkness was complete.

12

White skin drew out of the black. It stretched tight, pale and paper thin, over the frame of bones. Lucy lay on her side; she'd passed out on the floor of Todd Lowe's bedroom. The darkness watched her sleeping. It was just after 3:00am.

Lucy lay awkwardly on the stripped boards. She slept where the booze had left her. At some point she'd lost her shoes. Her bare feet huddled together for warmth. When the CTS Decon team had cleared the room they'd taken the carpet, too. The floorboards smelled of bleach; someone had been tasked with cleaning them, sponging Alex's blood into buckets.

Lucy had pulled her jacket half off while she slept. She'd been too hot and then too cold. Her blouse hung loosely; like her skin, it had fitted her once. Her neck had grown so thin that her veins bulged, ruddy worms snaking, just below the surface. It took in every detail of Lucy. Grief had stripped the life from her. She'd wasted away until she was a bag of bones, a dead thing unable to find peace.

Its gaze followed Lucy's skin, over her throat, across her jaw... It lingered on her face. Even in sleep the sadness that filled her every day shaped her expression.

Lucy stirred. The thing in the darkness retreated. It waited, until it was sure she hadn't woken, then it crept closer once more. Its attention turned to Lucy's hand, outstretched on the floorboards.

Lucy moaned. In the shapeless void of sleep, she could smell the bleach. It had crawled into her dream, turning the darkness red with blood. She was back in the tunnel, moving inevitably forward, desperately trying to stop herself, screaming to wake up...

And then she was awake. But it wasn't the thrashing in her dream that had woken her, it was a movement in the room with her! Her eyes snapped open.

"Alex?"

Lucy pulled herself up quick, the haze of sleep and booze immediately gone. Her eyes darted around the room, scanning the shadows for Alex's shape, for any movement that might signal she wasn't alone.

Something felt wrong. She pulled her jacket closed. That was when she noticed her hand.

 Painted across the fingers that had been outstretched on the floor was fresh plaster dust. Lucy caught her breath and got to her feet.

"Alex!" Could he really have been in the room just now? She stumbled from the bedroom and out into the hallway. What she saw stopped her in her tracks.

13

SKINNED FACES WATCHING

Lucy stood, frozen, in the doorway to Todd Lowe's room, her eyes fixed on the words carved into the wall ahead of her.

"Alex… Are you here?" she whispered.

Something sharp had been scored across the wall to spell out the message. Plaster, gouged from the wall, had been cast across the floor beneath the words. The same plaster she'd woken to find on her fingers?

This is wrong.

This is all wrong.

If the message was from Alex, why would he have written this?

Alex didn't write this.

No! She wouldn't believe that. She couldn't believe that. She'd contacted Alex! This was the sign, the proof she'd wanted. She'd called to him and he'd answered her. She just had to understand what it meant.

SKINNED FACES WATCHING

She balled her fists. If the message was from Alex, why was she shaking so badly? And why did she want to run?

She couldn't look at the words any longer. She turned away, squinting to see down the corridor, towards the wardrobe and the stairs. She could just make out more plaster scattered across the floor further down the hallway. A trail of plaster dust, stretching away from Todd's room like breadcrumbs leading her deeper into a nightmare.

"Alex?" Lucy whispered into the black.

Silence.

She managed to get up the nerve to step out from the doorway and into the hall. Her fists were white-knuckle tight. That hadn't stopped the shaking from spreading through her body. She gritted her teeth to try and stop them chattering.

As she got closer, she could see the letters in more detail. The S had been made from three strikes, driven downwards, tearing the plaster out of the wall. They made Lucy think of knife wounds. She'd touched the first message, had wanted to somehow connect with Alex through the letters. This time she kept her distance. The F in Faces had been scored so deep Lucy could see the brickwork beneath.

Lucy swiped the plaster dust from her fingers. She wanted it off her hands, off her skin. Her own fast movement, white skin flashing in the dark, almost set her running. She hurried across the hallway to get away from the words.

The lightless corridor was shapeless and endless. It seemed to slide over her as she moved along it. This what being swallowed alive feels like, she thought.

The second patch of plaster dust drew out of the shadows ahead of her, growing more defined as she closed on it. Lucy scanned the wall for any sign of another message. It seemed intact. Whoever had cut the words into the wall opposite Todd Lowe's room must have carried the dust on them to this point. The huge shape of the open wardrobe loomed in front of her.

To Lucy's left, the staircase dropped away into the hallway below. On weak, rubbery legs she approached the top stair. As she reached out a foot to step down, she felt the eyes burning into her back.

SKINNED FACES WATCHING.

Lucy swung out a shaking hand to grab for the bannister. Her fingers found the handrail and she gripped on. She stood, her breath rushing, her heart hammering, trying to work up the nerve to look over her shoulder. All the time she felt the eyes boring into her.

Slowly, Lucy turned to look into the gaping black mouth of the wardrobe. As she did, something smashed—glass smashed—loud in the darkness downstairs.

Lucy screamed and snapped back to the noise.

"Alex?" she pleaded. "Please, Alex, stop this. Mommy's really scared now."

The house had fallen silent once more.

Below, the light of a street lamp diffused through the stained-glass windows that framed the front door. Six squares of frail light painted onto the entrance hall floor. Six squares that looked as if the night might consume them at any moment.

Lucy began to descend the stairs. She had to know, no matter what waited in the shadows for her. As she reached the bottom step, the bannister on her right fell away and she stood, tiny against the huge darkness that filled the room. To her right, the light on her answering machine blinked, a chilling reminder of the rough voice caught in the hallway the previous night.

NO GOD

The sound of breaking glass had come from across the hall, in the lounge. She crossed the glowing squares, one unsteady step after another.

Get out! Get out now! The thought screamed into her mind. She could run, bolt for the door. Get out! Before it's too late! But she continued on, towards the lounge and whatever terrible revelation awaited her there, her shadow stretching back into the darkness beside her like a tether to the night. Until she had seen Alex, she was tied to this place.

14

The lounge door stood ajar. A sliver of solid black peeking in the gap between the painted white wood and the frame. The eye of a much larger beast beyond. Lucy was well aware that the living room had two doors, and that whatever had shattered the glass might have already left the living room by the other door, rounded on her by passing through the dining room or the kitchen, and back out into the hall. That it could have seen her crossing the hallway, masked in the deep shadows that surrounded her. Lucy turned away from the door.

And froze. Although she couldn't see, she had the overwhelming sense that she'd connected with another gaze in the dark, as if whatever watched her had silently drawn her eyes to the spot where it waited to be found.

Lucy squinted into the darkness. Now they'd locked gazes, what would it do next? Whatever was coming, she couldn't move. Fear had robbed her of any chance she might run.

The memory came out of the darkness at her first.

"Are you here? Are you there? Here I come… Hiders beware!" Hide and seek with Alex. They used to play for hours. He would hide and she would seek. He'd hide—they very rarely played with him as the seeker—then she'd close her eyes and count to fifty, listening to him moving around the house, settling on a spot, changing his mind, and then moving to a new hiding place. Once she'd hit fifty, she'd open her eyes and, with a voice she imagined a giant might boom *Fee Fie Foe*, she'd begin to call out her poem. "Are you here? Are you there? Here I come…

Hiders beware!"

Alex had been terrible at hiding, almost always giving himself away with a squeal of delight the moment she'd begin her poem. Lucy would happily play round after round to hear that joyous laugh and see the huge grin he wore from the first game they played to the last. Now, rooted to the spot in the dark, she sensed no joy at all from whatever watched her across the hallway.

Lucy opened her mouth to speak but all she managed was a fearful whimper. She tried again, trying to force the words out. The voice that followed was hoarse, shaking as badly as her body. "Are you here?" she called, her eyes searching the black ahead. "Are you there?" Everything was so terribly wrong. Still Lucy called the words into the darkness.

"Here I come…" Lucy took a step forward. When she played hide and seek with Alex, she would already be moving, hunting for him by the time she got to the final line of the poem. Hearing her moving about, he'd often begin giggling with excitement. The hallway remained silent. "Hiders beware." Lucy tried with all her heart to imagine her little boy waiting in the dark for her but, as she forced herself to take another step towards the thing that stared at her across the hallway, she grew more and more certain that it wasn't Alex.

15

Lucy stayed close to the wall, running the fingers of her left hand along the chalky plaster as she crossed the room with small, unsteady steps. All the time she could feel the unwavering stare fixed on her.

SKINNED FACES WATCHING

It didn't make sense that Alex would have written those words. Lucy knew him, knew the things that woke him in the night, knew his nightmares. Most times, the monsters in his closet were just the monsters he'd seen on TV. One time she'd woken to find him standing by her bedside whispering about a scary man muttering in the dark. It didn't take long for her to realize he'd had a nightmare about an old man they'd seen in the shopping mall earlier that day. Alex's monsters were literal, plucked from the world around him, the sort of spooks that should keep a seven-year-old up at night, not the awful mutilations that the messages evoked. Lucy had protected him, done everything she could to keep him from the darkness of the world.

Until that terrible night.

Her fingers pressed harder into the wall; harder still. She was no longer walking by the wall, it was holding her up.

And then it was gone. The wall disappeared so abruptly Lucy fell into the doorway. She screamed, grabbing blindly, catching handfuls of air, before managing to grab a hold of the doorframe with her right hand to stop her fall.

She clung to the frame, her heart slamming in her throat. The fall had spun her around. She'd lost her bearings.

And she'd lost track of the black stare.

Lucy whirled around to look behind her.

The hallway was empty. She could no longer feel the eyes burning into her. She scanned the shadows. If it had been Alex, why did she feel no warmth coming from it? If it had been Alex, why did she feel it was silently sizing her up, like an animal before it attacked?

Her watcher had disappeared back into the darkness that had birthed it. At least when she'd felt its stare she'd had some idea of where it might come at her from. Now everything further than a few feet around her was the same blurred black, a mass of shadows that could rush forward at any moment, forcing their black fingers into her throat, choking her screams.

16

Lucy stood in the living room doorway. The sound of breaking glass had come from this room. The weak glow of a distant streetlamp crept around the heavy curtains in the bay window. She listened. She couldn't hear the world outside. There didn't seem to be any glass at the foot of the curtains. The sound didn't seem to have been a window shattering.

Trying not to stumble, her hands sweeping a path in front of her, Lucy began to cross the room. As she reached forward she thought of herself in her nightmare. Of frightened fingers stretching out towards the broken boy.

The shape materialized in front of her at almost the same moment her hand brushed the thin frame. She snatched her hand back from the chair. She'd noticed the high-backed chair on the first evening, the way it faced the wall like a child being punished. Now it faced her. As if someone had sat watching, waiting for her to enter the room.

The seat was empty now.

Across the room, low to the ground, a glimmer caught Lucy's eye. Something flickered, silver on the floor ahead. Reluctantly, she stretched out her shaking hands once more and began to edge towards the light.

As she got closer she realized the flickering came from light reflecting on broken glass. This must be the source of the noise.

More pieces appeared. She stepped unsteadily onwards, trying to feel for shards before placing her bare feet down. More and more shards surrounded her feet, a black mosaic reflecting the night around her. The large mirror had fallen, or been torn, from the wall of the lounge. It lay face down on the floor.

Lucy knelt before it. The cord the mirror had hung from lay snapped in two across its back. Gently, she placed her fingers under the frame to lift the mirror up, then stopped.

Alex didn't do this.

She'd tried to silence the doubt, upstairs, in the hallway, but it was just getting louder and louder. A whisper growing to a scream.

She gripped the mirror's frame, sheets of broken glass shifting, grinding as she raised it from the boards.

You did this!
You reached into the darkness with all your heart,
and what have you pulled from it?

She lifted the mirror further, revealing her reflection, sliced a thousand times across the pieces of broken glass surrounding her. It revealed the room behind her, too.

Lucy leaned the mirror back against the wall. What she saw reflected made her cry out in horror.

Another message had been carved into the ceiling.

PEELED OPEN BELLY

"Oh no, oh no!"

The pieces of the mirror collapsed under their weight, falling from the frame, smashing on to one another, shattering with a huge noise that sent Lucy reeling backwards. She scrambled to get up, slipping, her bare feet sliding over the slivers of mirror. Broken glass sliced across the soles of her feet, tearing through the soft skin. She screamed, stumbling through the darkness, running for the doorway.

She heard glass break, a piece jammed in her foot snapping as she stepped down on it. She felt it shift and drive deep into the sole. The pain made her cry out. She buckled, throwing all her weight onto the other foot. She mustn't stop! If she stopped now, whatever waited in the darkness would find her. The grey-skinned thing that had lured her into the house would draw from the black, its body stinking of spoiled meat, ready to tear into her flesh the way it had scored its threats into the walls of the house.

She could feel the skin on her feet splitting as she ran. By the living room door, her box of cuttings had been upended, the paper she'd hoarded scattered across the floor. She ran over them, her blood staining the words that had driven her to madness.

...then he put the gun in his mouth

...kidnapper committed suicide

Lucy had bought 1428 Montgomery thinking that she might contact Alex, but Alex wasn't the only person who died that terrible night.

...killed himself

...monster found dead too

17

It listened to Lucy struggling to open the front door. She'd locked and bolted it to keep the world out, and now she was fighting against a trap of her own making. It listened as she shook the door in its frame, fumbling in the dark to slip the bolts she'd fastened.

Finally, she tore the door open, and she ran, her ripped feet slippery with blood, skidding and almost losing her footing on the frigid boards of the porch. She ran, her feet screaming as they pounded over the frozen ground. She ran until she fell against the side of her car.

Her hands shook so violently she could barely hold her car keys. She scored the paint, trying to jam the key into the lock.

Steadying one hand with the other, she finally drove the key home and tore open the door. She fell inside the car, slamming and locking the door behind her. Only then did she turn to look back at the house.

Darkness spilled from 1428 Montgomery, its shadow stretching over the lawn, over her car. Even now she wasn't safe from it! Lucy pulled her knees up to her chest—another barrier—her ruined feet resting on the edge of the seat. She thought she saw movement, in the doorway... The door rocking from where she'd ripped it open? On the night she'd seen the figure, she'd been able to make out the house clearly, but now, as if the darkness inside it had grown too large to contain, the front of the house was cloaked in black.

Lucy's panicked breathing blasted loud in the small space of her car. As she huddled, wide eyes darting manically over the black house, her breathing changed, snatched gasps that burned her throat into out of control sobbing. What had she done?

18

At the end of the corridor, like a hulking dark sentry, the wardrobe watched the stairs. Last night it had watched Lucy. She had sensed its glare, turned to look into its black mouth, before the sound of breaking glass had torn her away. Had she looked longer, she might have noticed the plaster dust gathered beneath the wardrobe, or the edges of the letters scored into the wall behind it.

No one had set foot in Anna Lowe's room since the removal company. Bob Taylor hadn't had to be at the house that day, but he'd watched as each room had been dismantled and packed into boxes. He'd made sure no one disturbed the curtains he'd drawn or tried to look into the room where Alex had died. He also made sure that everyone who entered the house had their ID checked. That morning, he'd stood in the lounge and watched Karen Guzman watching him from her car. He knew she'd take any opportunity to get into the house. He'd protect the families from the awful truth of that night for as long as he could.

Anna's room had no interest to Lucy. She only cared about the room where Alex had died. As far as she was concerned, the darkness was welcome to it.

In the corner of the room, low to the ground, where Anna's bed had stood, a series of rough letters had been scratched deep into the wall.

WaTCH you sLEEP

The shadow found Lucy asleep. She lay across the back seat of her car—knees still tucked up to her chest, her feet raw and glistening in the morning sun. Even after everything, she hadn't driven away. She couldn't leave 1428 Montgomery behind.

The shadow grew closer, stretching across the seat until it blocked out the sun. Lucy stirred but did not wake. And then someone was knocking loudly on the window.

Lucy leapt back away from the noise. She huddled in the corner of the back seat, wide eyed, her gaze fixed on the shadow pressing against the window.

What had she done? She hadn't meant to fall asleep! But she was just so exhausted! She'd watched the house for as long as she could, watched for the approach of the thing that had stalked her. She'd waited for its shadowy form to draw through the dead garden, to follow her to her hiding place in her car. The black figure tried the door handle.

She was helpless, a cornered animal.

"Lucy! Lucy! It's okay. It's me, Doctor Bachman."

Lucy didn't move.

"Lucy, what's happened? Please, open the door."

After a long moment, Lucy began to edge across the back seat, her eyes on the figure the whole time, afraid that once she got close enough she'd discover that it wasn't Doctor Bachman at all, but instead something grotesque wearing his skin.

Doctor Bachman had seen the wounds on Lucy's feet, the blood streaked across the back seat. He tried the door again.

"Lucy, it's okay. Please open the door."

Lucy's hand rested on the lock. She looked up to the shape in the window. The sun behind it hurt her eyes. It shifted, trying the door once more.

Hesitantly, Lucy unlocked it.

19

Doctor Bachman slowly opened the door, afraid that Lucy might bolt if he startled her again.

"Here, let me help you." He reached out a hand to Lucy.

Cautiously, she took it. It was warm. Not like the awful things that moved through the house. A wave of relief rushed through her. She started to cry.

"Lucy, it's okay. Whatever's happened, it's over now."

Gently, Doctor Bachman helped Lucy from the car. He put her arm over his shoulder, supporting her, taking the weight from her torn feet. If he'd been ten years younger, he would have offered to carry her. "Come on. Let's get you cleaned up."

They rounded the trunk and stood before the house. Lucy stopped.

"Are you alright?" Doctor Bachman followed Lucy's gaze. "You don't have to go back in there, you know. I can get someone to take a look at your feet at the hospital."

Lucy's eyes were fixed on the window of Todd Lowe's room.

Can you see me? Are you waiting for me?

"I have to."

They moved through the hallway, Doctor Bachman supporting Lucy— uninvited guests—two small figures swallowed by a beast neither could yet comprehend.

In the kitchen, Lucy had sat alone while Doctor Bachman returned to his car for supplies to treat her feet. She sat rigid, eyes fixed on the door, her hands gripping the edges of her seat until he returned.

When he did, he brought with him the spare sweater he kept in the car.

He handed it to Lucy.

"Here, put this on." Doctor Bachman could see his breath as he spoke. "They're forecasting snow this week." He ran his hand over the kitchen radiator. It was as cold as the rest of the house. "Where's the thermostat for your heating?"

Lucy couldn't answer that. She hadn't thought to look.

Doctor Bachman filled a bowl with warm water and knelt beside her. He gently wiped the clotted blood from Lucy's feet. She winced and gritted her teeth, ready for the pain to come. She'd pulled the largest shards from her feet while she'd been locked in the car, parting the slits of skin and working the pieces out. But the smaller ones, the ones too deep or too painful for her fingers to grasp, remained. Doctor Bachman rinsed the cloth. Lucy's blood melted into the water, streaks spiralling to fading trails. Fragments of glass glimmered as they sank to the bottom of the bowl.

The house creaked. Doctor Bachman felt Lucy start. Her head snapped up. She watched the ceiling with wide eyes. "What on earth happened, Lucy?"

She thought before answering.

"I dropped a mirror," she lied.

"Last night?"

Lucy nodded.

"What were you doing with it?"

Lucy avoided Doctor Bachman's gaze. She'd always been honest with him. She hated not telling him everything. "It'd fallen off the wall."

"You dropped it, or it fell?"

"No, I... It just fell. I didn't drop it."

Doctor Bachman smiled warmly, "You know, all that bad luck stuff? It's just superstition, nothing to worry about."

Lucy didn't smile back. "I still don't believe in that sort of thing."

Doctor Bachman returned to tending to her wounds. With a pair of tweezers, he pulled the shards he could reach from the raw slices in her feet.

"There are some pieces of glass I can't get to. You're going to have to have them removed at the hospital. I can make you an appointment today when I'm at the General if you'd like."

Lucy watched the doorway behind Doctor Bachman.

"Matt said you'd seen Alex here."

She looked back down to him.

"I think so."

"Is that why you bought the house?"

Lucy nodded. Doctor Bachman rested a gauze dressing on the edge of the bowl. The water was pink with Lucy's blood.

"Have you seen him again since?

Lucy looked away. A tear streaked her cheek.

"It's okay, Lucy."

"No, no it's not!"

Lucy planted her hands on the kitchen table and used it to take her weight as she pulled herself up. "Come with me."

Tottering on her injured feet, Lucy led Doctor Bachman to the lounge door. It was shut. She hesitated. "I don't remember closing..." Last night she'd run terrified from the living room. She hadn't closed the door behind her.

She leaned in towards the door, listening for the slightest sound from the living room. The house was silent. She took a deep breath to try and calm her nerves. It didn't work. Slowly she turned the handle and pushed the door open.

She could see her cuttings scattered across the floor, the words that had drawn her to the black house now stuck together with her blood.

Enough morning light bled around the curtains to pick out a trail of broken glass leading across the room.

Doctor Bachman followed Lucy, stepping carefully, avoiding the pieces of bloody mirror that traced Lucy's frantic escape from the house.

As they crossed the room, Doctor Bachman noticed the high-backed chair drawing out of the gloom. He wondered why Lucy would have positioned it facing the wall like that. He tried to focus on following her but the chair pulled his gaze back. He grew increasingly uneasy that he couldn't see if someone was sitting in it.

"Look." Lucy's words made the doctor start. He turned to see her pointing up to the ceiling. "I found this last night. I... I've no idea how it got there."

PEELED OPEN BELLY

"There are more of them."

This was far worse than anything Doctor Bachman had imagined.

"Lucy, how...?"

Lucy fumbled for words to explain.

"I did it! I bought the house to try and contact Alex. After I'd seen him, upstairs in that room, I swore I'd do anything to get a message from him."

PEELED OPEN BELLY

"I don't know what I've done, but it's bad. It's really bad! Whoever wrote this, wrote these messages, they're evil, insane."

Doctor Bachman was furious with himself. How could he have let this happen?

"You have to leave this house, Lucy."

"No!" Lucy backed away from the doctor. Shards of broken mirror crowded her bare feet. "I can't! Don't you see? If I've contacted someone, something, I have to keep trying. Doesn't this mean that it's possible at least that I might contact Alex?"

"Lucy, listen to me. I'm a scientist. I don't believe in ghosts. I do believe in monsters but they're human beings like you and me. If someone is doing this, writing these messages, then you need to be as far away from them as possible. I want you to pack a bag. Lucy, come to the hospital tonight. You'll be safe there."

Lucy shook her head. "I can't do that."

"You have to. Look, I've got appointments at the General today. You can come with me."

Lucy's eyes darted from Doctor Bachman up to the scrawled threat carved above her. She wanted to go, wanted to run, but while there was any chance at all that she might contact Alex, she had no choice but to stay.

"I can't."

Doctor Bachman edged back. Lucy's feet shifted. There was a wildness in her eyes, an unpredictable fear. He was afraid that if he kept pressing her she might bolt, panic and run across the pieces of the mirror.

"I'm sorry, Lucy, I've got to go now but I'll be done by three. Pack a bag. I'll come back and collect you." Doctor Bachman made to leave the living room. He looked back at Lucy. "Please trust me. You mustn't stay here another night."

As Doctor Bachman descended the overgrown path he felt the gaze on his back. He turned, expecting to see Lucy standing in the doorway, hoping she'd changed her mind and would come to the hospital with him after all. But the doorway was empty. He must have been mistaken. He tried to laugh at himself—he'd let Lucy's ghost story get under his skin. But, if that was the case, why did he feel the same sick unease he'd felt in the living room when he'd seen the high-backed chair? He pulled his coat closed. He was shaking. Even though he'd left the house, its creeping cold remained with him.

20

Doctor Bachman switched on the heating and wound the dial to the hottest setting. He reached into his jacket and pulled out a pack of *Marlboro*. He tapped the pack on his leg until a smoke stood out far enough for him to grab it between his teeth. He lit it and clicked on the radio. *Golden Gate Greats*. He hoped the music and the nicotine would help calm his nerves.

As he drove, he felt warm air beginning to rush over the back of his hand on the wheel. He angled the vents to get the full benefit of the heating. Doctor Bachman drew deeply on his smoke. He tried to dismiss the unease he'd felt in the house—it was just the guilt he felt over Lucy's situation, the concern that had been growing ever since she'd left the hospital. No, there was more to it than that. He kept returning to that chair. He wondered what would have happened if he'd continued on, rounded its high back. What black thing would have waited for him there?

The words had been carved into the wall with such force that they were scored right down to the brick.

NEVER OVER

As Doctor Bachman put some distance between himself and the house he began to relax. Eventually the stream of hot air blasting from the car's heater became stifling. He wasn't ready to switch it off, so he wound down the window. Even though his face and hands felt flushed, he couldn't rid himself of the cold that had lingered at his back ever since he'd gotten into the car.

Rush hour had passed and the roads outside the city were quiet. Doctor Bachman lit another cigarette off his last, something he hadn't found himself doing for years. He was driving too fast, worried about Lucy. He had to get her out of that house. If she wouldn't leave when he returned from the General, he'd look into getting an order for an involuntary commitment. Alex's death had utterly destroyed her. If she remained at the house the consequences could be terrible. How could he have let the situation spiral so far out of control?

He threw his half-smoked cigarette out of the window. He shouldn't have lit it in the first place. The nicotine made him feel shaky and nauseous. He leaned back in his seat. As he did, the cold that had followed him from the house closed around him.

He heard his seat belt unlocking. He looked down to see what was happening. In the same instant the belt was ripped upwards. It caught on his jaw, jerking his head back, before pulling taut around his throat.

21

Doctor Bachman tore at the belt, his nails gouging his throat as he fought to force his fingers between the seat belt and his neck. The car swerved out across the road.

He groped frantically for the wheel, managing to catch a hold of it with a flailing hand. He jerked it back, swinging the car out of the oncoming lane. All the time, the belt was pulled tighter from behind. He stamped blindly in the foot well, trying to find the brake. His foot found the accelerator instead.

The car tore forward over the brow of the hill and launched into the air. Doctor Bachman dropped the wheel, throwing his hands up in front of his face, bracing…

Moments later the car slammed back to earth, metal scraping, sparking on the asphalt. The impact threw the Doctor forward, his whole weight straining against his trapped neck. He felt the muscles in his throat tearing, and howled in agony.

The car fishtailed, the back end spinning out. It skidded sideways into the oncoming traffic in the junction at the foot of the hill.

Only then was the belt around his neck released.

The woman in the SUV didn't have time to react as Doctor Bachman's car swung into her path. She slammed head on into his passenger side door. The door buckled and caved—metal and glass punched into the cabin. The sudden, dead stop ripped Doctor Bachman from his seat, hurling him towards the passenger door.

The seat belt snapped taut and locked. Doctor Bachman was jerked back with such force he slammed into the half open window, smashing his collar bone and shattering the window into a glass spider's web.

For a moment everything was black.

In the dream, it was trying to strangle him, grey skin, putrid, it stank of oil and rotten meat. Its glass fingers scraped at his neck, tightening around his throat, scratching, tearing. Blood was pouring over the glass.

Doctor Bachman opened his eyes. He could still feel the cold around his throat. The force of the collision had left him slumped, his head hanging out of the driver's side window. His neck lay on the shattered pane: he could feel it digging into his throat. He tried to move but couldn't lift his head. The cold around his throat was his blood.

He felt the glass shifting, the weight of his head pressing his throat down on the jagged edge of the shattered window. The veins in his neck bulged, swelling over the pane.

As he lay helpless, he heard a car speeding down the hill towards him.

The Audi driver had been talking on his cell. He saw the accident too late. Now he hammered on the brake, tires screaming.

Doctor Bachman closed his eyes.

Christ, let it be over quickly.

The Audi skidded down the hill, closer and closer.

And then it stopped. The bumper nudged against Doctor Bachman's driver side door. He could feel the heat of the car's engine radiating through its hood. He whimpered—a sigh of relief that smoked and faded on the freezing air.

Doctor Bachman raised a trembling hand to grab for the door handle, trying to get some leverage to pull his neck from the broken window. He could feel the two halves of his snapped collar bone shifting beneath his skin, scraping awkwardly against one another. Every small move was agony.

A large splinter of metal, shrapnel from the mangled passenger door, had been driven into Doctor Bachman's wrist in the crash. It had sliced through the cuff of his shirt, cutting deep into the flesh beneath. Blood trickled over his fingers as he felt across his door.

He found the handle, closed his wet fingers into a fist around it, then pushed down, trying to lift his weight.

Doctor Bachman's wrist snapped with a sickening crack. He screamed as the bone shattered, bursting through his skin and slamming forward into the electric window control above the door handle. The window started to life, beginning to rise in its frame.

He screamed for help, stretching his neck as much as he could but the broken glass dug into his skin. Then it was slicing into his throat. The pieces of the pane cracked loudly, forced together as they drove through the cords of muscle.

Doctor Bachman twisted, desperately trying to dislodge his forearm, but the dead weight of his broken body held it wedged against the switch.

His jugular swelled around the rising pane.

"No! No! Plea—"

Then it split, thick blood jetting down the door. Outside, a woman was screaming. "Call 911! Someone call 911!"

Then the window jammed.

The motor driving the pane cycled, locking, slipping back, locking, slipping back, trying to drive through the vertebra. The glass crackled, shaking, compacting, the window jolting forward and jerking back again.

With an awful snap, the window was free. It sliced through the remaining sinew of Doctor Bachman's neck. The last cords of muscle and skin stretched and split.

Doctor Bachman's body slumped lifeless against the shattered window. His head landed on the hood of the Audi.

The window fully closed.

22

There was nothing that stood out about the house, no detail to define it, no reason to pull it from the other houses in the quiet street. Nor was there anything about the small woman in her late fifties, standing, watching from the single glazed window, that would cause anyone to pull her from a crowd.

It had been raining for almost an hour. The clouds that had predicted snow had instead brought freezing rain. Lucy was soaked through. She barely noticed. She wasn't sure what she'd expected, but it wasn't this.

Emma had no idea how long Lucy had been standing outside her house. She'd only spotted her twenty minutes ago when she'd pulled herself from the couch to refill her glass. She'd known this day would come. Still, she wasn't prepared at all. Her hands shook so badly she could hear her glass rattling on the sill where she rested it. She put down the empty glass and disappeared from the window.

A few moments later, she appeared at the front door holding an umbrella. She crossed the street to where Lucy stood. Emma opened the umbrella and held it over Lucy to protect her from the rain.

Eventually, they returned to the house together. Lucy stopped at the threshold. Emma didn't rush her. She waited, patiently shielding Lucy from the freezing downpour, until she was ready to head inside. After a time, Lucy took the final steps up into the kidnapper's house.

The first thing Lucy noticed was the silence. It hung heavy over the hallway, and filled the lounge where Emma led her to an armchair to sit. The same muted agony that followed Lucy everywhere she went. Without speaking, Emma left the room and Lucy alone.

Lucy could taste the dust in the air. A blanket lay across the sagging couch. An empty vodka bottle sat on the carpet, within arm's reach of the couch.

Emma returned and handed Lucy a towel.

She didn't use it. Instead, she placed it on the arm of her chair. Like everything in Emma Roberts' house, it smelt of dust, of another life that had ended on that terrible April night.

Emma sat on the couch opposite Lucy: two mothers who had lost their sons, wrapped in the silence of their grief. Lucy studied Emma. She sat with her hands clasped together in her lap. Her head was bowed. Long strands of grey hair had escaped her loose pony tail and spilled across her soft features. She hid behind them. She looked exhausted. Emma's eyes flickered up and found Lucy. When their gazes connected, she tried to force a small smile to put Lucy at ease. What had Lucy expected? That his mother would be a monster too? That somehow seeing her would explain how he had come to be the thing he was? Looking at Emma now, Lucy only saw her own pain. She recognized the empty look in Emma's eyes. She saw herself in twenty years' time, and had to turn away.

Across the mantlepiece and walls, photographs of a happy family filled frame after frame. A proud mother and father posing with their young son, a toddler—squinting, the sun in his eyes—surrounded by sandcastles. First Christmas, first bike, year after year, photographs charted a happy childhood. The kidnapper had been a monster by the time he'd taken Alex; but he hadn't always been that way.

As the boy became a man, the happy images became less frequent, until they ran out altogether.

"His father left six months after he started getting sick." Emma's voice was quiet, hoarse. Like Lucy, she barely spoke anymore. She reached into her pocket and took out a worn photograph.

"It was only after he died, I realized I'd only taken one picture of him in the past fifteen years."

She looked down at the image, taking it in one more time, before carefully handing it to Lucy. "I guess we only take pictures of the times we want to remember."

In the photograph Alex's kidnapper smiled, his arm around his mom, hugging her. Emma looked tired but happy. "He was on his medication then. We went to the zoo. He was my boy again".

Lucy couldn't look at the picture. She handed it gently back to Emma.

"I'm sorry. I shouldn't have come." Lucy began to pull herself to her feet.

Emma's words pressed her back into the chair.

"I tried to get him put into the hospital but they wouldn't listen to me. They said as long as he took his medication he'd be okay at home."

Emma looked up from the photograph; her eyes full of tears. "But, he wouldn't keep up his pills. Every time they started working he thought he was cured and stopped. I begged him to carry on. At first, he'd just say I was wrong, then, as he got sick again, he'd accuse me of plotting against him, of being part of some plan... He thought I was trying to poison him!"

Lucy had wanted to hate Emma for what her son had done, but she couldn't.

"I kept calling the hospital, trying to get something done for him. They put him on a register, said someone would come and check up on him. They never did. He just got worse and worse. It was so black, the things he'd say... So horrible, things I couldn't imagine."

Emma gently returned the photograph to her pocket. The son she'd loved was not the man she was talking about now. Tears began to spill down her cheeks.

"I had no idea he'd do what he did. There were times when I stayed up with him all night because I was afraid he might hurt himself, but not anyone else. Not anyone else. I'm so sorry for what he did to your son."

The words made Lucy want to scream—a raw vein of complete despair that she fought to keep under control, clawing to tear from her body. She clenched her hands into fists, dug her fingernails into the palms of her hands.

She'd wanted answers. She'd come looking for some kind of revenge. She'd hidden a knife in her jacket. But, sitting opposite this utterly broken mother, all she felt was empathy—a sickening, overwhelming empathy.

"It wasn't your fault." Lucy watched Emma quietly crying, her own face cold with her tears. It won't ever be over, she thought. This is all the future holds for me.

After a time, Emma got to her feet. She crossed the living room to an old roll-top dresser. She opened the top drawer and removed a book. A brown moleskin notebook.

She handed the book to Lucy. "He wrote in this when he was ill. Kept it hidden. He thought I didn't know where he kept it. I'm his mother, of course I knew. I'm not ready to look at it yet. Maybe it will help you, though."

Lucy looked down at the journal in her hands. What Emma had said was still sinking in.

"I'll make some coffee."

Emma left Lucy alone.

Lucy suddenly felt very weak. She half placed, half dropped the scuffed, thumbed journal onto the arm of the chair. She wanted it out of her hands. Touching something that *he* had touched made her feel sick.

When she'd stood watching Emma's house, crazed thoughts squirming through her mind, she'd convinced herself that the knife in her jacket pocket, the knife she'd gripped with white knuckles, might help her wrestle back some kind of control. She had no plan further than that.

She hadn't expected Emma's kindness, nor had she expected that *his* house would hold a broken reflection of herself. Now, looking down at *his* journal on the arm of her seat, Lucy felt she'd walked into a trap. The illusion of control that had lured her here was gone, replaced with the same terror that had sent her running from 1428 Montgomery.

The silence she'd taken for mourning had closed in around her. Now it was the silence before a scream.

23

The book was thick with his words. Even without opening it, Lucy could see that almost every page in the journal had been written on. Every fibre of her wanted to throw it across the room, rip it into little pieces, show it the same rage she'd show *him* if he'd been standing in front of her. Instead, she sat soundless and still.

Touching the journal was like touching something dead. Its cold, rough skin made Lucy snatch her fingers back. Her head was pounding, nausea rising into her throat. Had he written about Alex before he'd taken him, before he'd killed him?

This is what they'd all tried to protect her from. Matt, Bob Taylor, even Doctor Bachman. They'd obscured the truth, wrapped it in a series of half lies for her sake. But she needed to know, needed to know every single detail to try to make some sense of what had happened. They were Alex's last moments—her last moments—and all their well-intentioned avoidance had just nurtured the madness that writhed inside her.

So, when Guzman had published her lurid account of Alex's murder, Lucy hadn't hated her for it. After all, she'd been the only one to tell Lucy the truth. The only one to give her the details she'd needed, no matter how devastating they were. But it was already too late for Lucy. By then the whispering had taken hold.

Two weeks ago, Lucy had been sitting on the painted white chair at the painted white table in room 23b at the William Tuke Psychiatric Hospital when a letter had arrived for her. It wasn't signed, but it wasn't the first handwritten note she'd received from Karen Guzman. It simply read:

This is where he came from.

And Emma Roberts' address had followed. Two days later, Lucy had checked herself out of the hospital.

Lucy picked up the book: his book. After everything she'd done, she couldn't fail Alex now. No matter how much it repulsed her, no matter what terrible secrets lay within the journal, she had to read it, had to face the man who had murdered her son.

24

No more.

Emma felt the metal, cold against her temple. It surprised her, made her want to pull her head away. She looked out of the kitchen window, out at the heavy rain streaking the glass. The moment she'd put the photograph back into her pocket, she'd lost his face. Recently, if she wasn't looking at the photograph, she had trouble pulling an image of him from her memory. The details were distorted, as if she were trying to recall a stranger, not her own son. She knew there was a part of her, so tired, so ashamed, that wanted to forget him. That part grew every day and she hated herself for not stopping it. In truth, she didn't want to, and it was that truth that had led her to the end.

She'd thought that, when the time came, she might be thinking of him. Instead she found herself hoping the rain would stop for Lucy's sake. Emma closed her eyes.

In that moment, all that existed was the sound of the gunshot. It tore through Emma Roberts' small house like a huge and furious animal. It stole the scream from Lucy's lips, drowning her horrified cry in its terrible noise.

The journal dropped from Lucy's hands. A loud crack from the kitchen, the gun clattering onto the tiles, was followed by the sound of the dead weight of Emma's body thudding to the ground.

Then there was an awful quiet.

A sob burst from Lucy's lips. She gripped the arms of the chair, trying to hear over the sound of her own hitching breaths, desperate for a sound, any sound, to reassure her that what she dreaded was wrong.

No sound came.

She couldn't breathe, couldn't get her breathing under control. All the air had been sucked out of the room. She pulled herself out of the chair, she swayed on her legs and almost collapsed. She managed to stumble to the lounge doorway. There, she clung onto the doorframe to hold herself up, "Please...!" She coughed the words, gasping for the air to speak.

The door to the kitchen was ajar. From where Lucy stood she could see the tiled floor. She could see the gun. The acrid taste of gunpowder caught in the back of her throat. She could smell burnt hair, seared skin. Had she done this? Had she caused this? Darkness was bleeding into her peripheral vision. Lucy gripped the frame so tightly the wood cut into her fingers.

"Emma? Emma, please!"

The hallway was shrinking as she staggered towards the kitchen. Growing darker. Like the tunnel to the broken boy. This had always been the killer's home. He'd lived in it until he'd taken his own life. Had run through this hallway as a child, raced into the kitchen, to Emma's side, watched her peeling vegetables for Sunday dinner, waiting for her to turn and smile. No! No, that was Lucy, that was *her* mother, standing at the sink peeling carrots in the house where she grew up. She could see her, see her smile. *Why can't you be here now?*

Why does everything have to be so wrong?

Please make it stop.

Make it stop!

The darkness was spreading, black hands now reaching across her eyes. She fell against the wall.

She was close enough now to see the blood.

Deep red on the bone-white tiles, Emma's blood swelled towards the kitchen doorway: a growing pool pumped from her shattered skull by her dying heart. Ripples spread through the blood, the waves growing weaker as the thick fluid stretched towards Lucy.

From the direction of the blood, she could tell Emma's body must have fallen just behind the kitchen door. She could see Emma's feet now, her legs appearing. Unable to stop herself, Lucy leaned forward to look around the door.

25

At the last moment, Emma had tried to turn away from the gun. The impact of the bullet punching through the back of her skull had thrown her into the cabinets that lined her small kitchen. She'd whirled around, as metal and bone corkscrewed through the tissue of her brain, turning almost a full circle before slamming the hollowed out remains of her head down onto the worktop and slumping down on the tiled floor below.

In the living room, Lucy had been struck by Emma's kind features. Now those features were gone. Emma's face ended abruptly just above her top lip.

Lucy clung onto the kitchen door, but her fingers were slipping…

The darkness blinked in.

Emma's left hand lay open by her side, an island of pale skin drowning in her blood.

Lucy's fingers lost their grip. She was falling.

Falling into the black.

Into nothing.

For a moment it was all gone.

Emma's obliterated face.

The blood and bone cast high over the kitchen walls.

Only the darkness existed.

And in it she was safe. Safe from the horror.

Safe from the unending grief.

And Alex was there, too.

She could feel him reaching out to her.

Alex, I love you so much.

She could feel him drawing closer.

The cold coming closer.

Why are you so cold?

She felt him touch her face.

Can I stay here?

Please, God, let me stay here.

Plea... Her knees slammed down on the kitchen tiles. The pain jolted her awake. She was back, falling into the blood, knees first, now her upper body was toppling forward over Emma's corpse.

She threw her hands out to stop herself, planting them down on Emma's legs. She screamed, immediately wanting to snatch them back, propel herself backwards, away from the body, but she was too weak. Instead, she knelt over Emma, sobbing, begging to be swallowed back into the darkness again.

Emma's blood seeped into the material of Lucy's trousers.

Eventually, she found the strength to lift her head, and rocked backward so she was sitting on the kitchen floor. She brought her hands up to wipe the tears from her face. She stopped when she saw they were covered in Emma's blood.

Across from where Lucy sat, on the other side of Emma's body, was a patch of the tiled floor where no blood had run. It had spread around the space, but the shape it outlined remained clean. It made Lucy think of a bone jutting out from a wound.

As she pulled herself back to her feet, she thought it was her shadow she saw moving across the kitchen wall.

It wasn't.

The blood smeared, something sliding on it as it moved across the tiles. Lucy screamed. She saw its shadow unravelling on the wall in front of her. Whatever the blood had spilled around, whatever unseen thing had crouched by Emma's body, now climbed to its feet. Lucy could feel the terrible cold that radiated from it, reaching out towards her.

She stumbled wildly backwards, twisting to get away. Her feet skidded in Emma's blood and she was sent crashing into the wall. The impact punched the air from her lungs and she collapsed, half through the kitchen doorway.

She lay on her side, wheezing, frantically trying to suck in enough air to pull herself back to her feet. Lucy's eyes darted over the doorway.

Where is it?

Her legs trailed into the kitchen behind her.

Where is it?

She was sure it was the same terrible cold that had pinned her to the bed in her apartment, and she was sure if it caught her now she would never leave Emma's house.

Lucy kicked her legs into the air: a futile attempt to fend off the thing. She could feel the cold gaining on her, pulling at her ankles as she lashed out. At any moment that pull would become a grip, and then it would have her.

She rolled onto her front. Grabbing handfuls of carpet, she managed to scramble onto all fours. Less than an hour ago the hallway had been heavy with silence, now it echoed with the blasting sound of her panic.

She crawled along the hallway. Had it followed her from 1428 Montgomery? Had the thing she'd dragged from the darkness with her Ouija board followed her here? Had *he* returned home?

She was an easy target, easy prey: exhausted, struggling to breathe, hauling herself along the floor. She could feel the cold advancing, gaining on her. One thought pushed her forward: if she didn't get out of here, if she didn't get away from here, she'd never see Alex again.

She staggered to her feet, and slid along the wall, leaning into it for support. She snatched a look behind her. It was there, she could feel it, the way she had felt Alex in the darkness, unseen but close. She fell against the front door, fumbling for the lock.

26

Lucy tore open the door and ran, stumbling down the wet steps from the unremarkable house on the unremarkable street. The sudden cold of the freezing rain stung her face, shocking the darkness from her sight. Emma's last wish had not come true.

Lucy ran, without looking back, until she hit the side of her car. She'd torn the dressings Doctor Bachman had applied to her sliced feet. Her shoes felt wet inside. She could feel the blood squelching in her socks. There was pain too, but only faintly, fear and adrenaline keeping it at arm's length for now.

She shut the passenger side door and slammed her hand down on the locking pin. Rain drummed on the roof of the car. Her fast breathing fogged the windows. She wiped her hand over the glass so she could see. Her fingers left a trail of Emma's blood behind them. She watched Emma's house. How could she hide from something she couldn't see?

She started the engine and pulled away from the curb. She drove fast, too fast. The roads were icy, the freezing rain turning to sleet as night reached in from across the bay.

Lucy drove for hours. She drove in circles. She thought about driving to the William Tuke Psychiatric Hospital. She drove until the car was running on fumes. Then, she drove back to the house.

27

Doctor Bachman didn't return. Lucy waited for him. She waited until her car ran out of gas and fell silent. Then she waited on the street. She stood where the children had raced, wailing across the overgrown front lawn. She stood before the house, small and vulnerable.

She watched the upstairs windows for any sign of the grey figure that had first drawn her inside. What if it hadn't been Alex? What if it hadn't *ever* been Alex?

Knotted grass twined around her ankles as she crossed the lawn. Was it trying to stop her, or maybe hold her in the house's shadow long enough that it could study its catch before devouring it?

Lucy stepped up onto the porch. She noticed the door immediately. It was ajar.

I knew you'd come back.

She stepped hesitantly across the slick boards.

Closer, closer, come closer.

This was her last chance to turn around. Whatever lay within the house had let her leave once; she was sure it would not let that happen again.

She remembered the words she'd spoken, that first night after she'd left the hospital: "Doctor Bachman says I shouldn't come here. Well, where else am I supposed to go?" There was a terrible finality in those words now. She started to laugh. An awful sound that bubbled up from inside her, that clawed its way out, broken and full of fear. So dark, that when it left her mouth, she was surprised it wasn't a scream.

Lucy pressed the front door open, pressed it back into the black that lay beyond. And then she followed it.

She tried to be quiet, tried to be small, to go unnoticed as she stepped painfully across the dim hallway towards the stairs. She clung to the wall as she climbed the staircase. If she pressed herself into it, maybe she wouldn't be seen. If she stepped lightly, maybe she wouldn't be heard.

When she reached the top of the stairs the stench was waiting for her. The stink of rancid meat. It grew stronger with every unsteady, frightened step she took towards Todd Lowe's room. She followed the wall through the darkness. She could feel the wounds on her feet spreading open, sharp pain flaring, each time she put any weight on them. The memory of broken glass tearing into her soles played over and over in her mind. Only now she saw it slicing through the fingers that traced the wall, now it scraped across her belly, now it flashed out of the shadows at her eyes— her fingers grazed the letters carved into the plaster: **SKINNED FACES WATCHING.** She snatched her hand away.

The door to Todd Lowe's room was shut. Lucy closed her fingers around the freezing handle.

As she opened the door, she started to scream.

28

"Oh no! No, no, no!" The Ouija board had been hurled at the wall. It lay broken, underneath the rough plaster where Alex had died. But that was not what made Lucy cry out.

In the centre of the room lay Alex's case. What was left of it. The case had been smashed open, its clasps shattered. The lid had been ripped from the bottom half, its leather stretched, skin pulled taut till it tore.

The contents of Alex's case had been cast around the room. His books had had their spines snapped, their pages torn out and shredded. His clothes had been ripped limb from limb. The red sweater Lucy had treated with such reverence had been gutted, sliced up the middle and peeled open.

"No, no, no!"

She dropped to her knees and began frantically trying to scoop up Alex's things. His books fell to pieces in her hands, her fingers slipped through the tears in his clothes. She grabbed Alex's Action Jack figure from the floor. As she turned it over she dropped it in horror.

The doll's skull had been cracked open. Where its eyes should have been, empty sockets glared at Lucy. The face bulged, stretched and deformed. Its limbs had been twisted and pulled from its torso.

Lucy snatched the case from the floor, her arms filled with the broken remains of Alex's things.

She stuffed all the pieces—the torn paper, the ruined clothes, the smashed and broken toys—back into the case, trying hopelessly to put everything back how it had been.

The lid was too damaged to close.

She held the sides of the case together but Alex's things spilled from its ripped open body.

Everything she'd hoarded, protected. Everything she had left of Alex had been destroyed. She cradled the remains to her and she screamed. A terrible, desolate wail.

"*Why? Why have you done this?*"

She screamed again and again, her pitiful cries echoing through the house as the last piece of Lucy to survive her grief left her. The last breath of her dying mind, gone into the squirming void that had been at her back ever since Alex had been slaughtered.

It fizzed and burned out.

Like a filament in a bulb.

Flaring and disintegrating.

Irreparable.

29

She might have sat there for an hour, maybe two, weeping and rocking the broken case in her arms. In the end, it was the scent of him that pulled her back. Faint, fading from the shredded clothes she clung to. It was the scent of him that pulled her across the room, to the foot of the wall where the broken Ouija board lay.

"It's okay, Mommy's here." Her voice was hollow. Something had gone from it, never to return.

She gathered up the pieces of the broken board. The planchette was nowhere to be seen.

She placed the pieces together on top of the shattered case. She stretched out her middle and index fingers and rested her hand gently in the centre of the board. She would be the planchette.

"Alex, it's me. It's Mommy." She whispered, afraid the kidnapper might hear her. "Can you hear me, Alex?"

Her fingers remained still in the middle of the board.

"Don't be afraid." She leaned over the board, shielding it from the darkness around her. "If you can talk to me, say something. I *need* to hear from you… I need…"

Gently, slowly, Lucy's hand began to move across the board. She followed her fingers as they came to rest on the letter *P*.

Had she done that? Had the movement simply been her willing her hand to move, desperate for a message from Alex?

She felt a tug at her wrist, her hand being guided across the board once more. A letter *O* followed the *P*. Then another *O* and an *R*. **POOR**. Next her hand was led to a *D*, then an *E* and back to *D*. **DED**. *B, O, Y*. **BOY**. An *H* then an *A*, another *H, A, H, A, H, A*. **Ha, Ha, Ha.**

Lucy called out, "For God's sake! Stop this! Please! I just want to talk to Alex! Why are you doing this? Why did you have to ruin his things? They were all I had left of him!"

Her hand began to move again. *P*, then *L*, *A* then *Y*, *I*, *N*. **PLAYIN**.

"Playing? You're playing with me? You killed my son, you fuck! You're a monster! You hear me? A monster!"

Lucy tried to hold her hand still, didn't want to hear what *he* had to say next, but the force that dragged her was too strong. *Y*, then *O*, *U*, *R*. **YOUR**. *M*, *O*, *N*, *S*, *T*, *E*, *R*. **MONSTER**.

She clamped her free hand over her wrist, fought to wrestle her hand from the board. "No!" But *his* grip was too powerful. He'd found a way to be heard and he was going to make her listen.

H, *E*, *A*, *R*. **HEAR**

H, *E*, *A*, *R*. **HEAR**

HEAR what?

"I don't want to hear what you have to say!"

H, *E*, *A*, *R*.

H, *E*, *A*, *R*.

Lucy's fingers tore across the board, letter to letter, the grip getting tighter, stronger.

I, *M*.

I, *M*.

I, *M*, *H*, *E*, *A*, *R*. **I'M HEAR!**

Suddenly, her hand was released. She snatched it away from the board. I'M HERE!

Lucy froze. The bedroom had grown darker, shadows had stolen in and surrounded her while she'd been distracted.

Then she felt it, behind her.

"Please, no."

The words fell from her lips. It wasn't Alex. She was sure of that. It couldn't be. Whatever lurked in the darkness meant to hurt her. She shouldn't have come back here.

The stench wrapped around her. In her peripheral vision, she saw the darkness shift. At the last moment she turned to look. That was when the black thing pounced, the rotten carcass grabbing her, throwing her over, slamming her head into the floor with such force she was knocked out.

30

The scream tore out of the darkness. It jolted Matt from a thin and anxious sleep. He knew immediately that something was terribly wrong. The scream came again. His cell phone drummed angrily on the bedside table. He fumbled for the phone and answered it. He wasn't thinking, he just wanted the screaming to stop.

It wasn't the first time that Matt had been woken by screaming in the night.

About a month after Lucy had left, Matt had started awake at 4:00am. At first, he wasn't sure what had woken him. He'd lain in the dark, listening, unable to fathom why he'd woken in fright. Then he'd heard it.

Faint, off in the distance, an injured animal cried for help.

He guessed it was coming from the woods that surrounded the house. It sounded like a deer, or maybe a fox, caught in the trap. What he could hear, even at a distance, was the desperation in each howl, it was a miserable sound. The sound of something dying.

Matt had gotten out of bed. He'd stood in front of the large living room windows. He could see the edge of the woods, the treeline bordering his driveway. He'd watched, waiting, expecting to see the wounded animal stumble from the cover of the trees, buckling and falling onto the wet earth. No movement came.

Still the wailing sound continued.

The longer he heard it, the more it unnerved him. He'd stepped back away from the glass, moved through the house, but the sound had followed him. No matter where he stood, he could hear it. He'd begun to dread each cry, each pitiful howl. Eventually he couldn't stand it anymore and he'd grabbed his car keys, headed into the garage and gotten into the Camaro.

There he'd locked himself in, gripping the wheel with clenched fists as the garage door had risen, inch by inch, revealing the dark landscape ahead.

Matt drove slowly along the driveway. The knot of anxiety that had made him step back from the living room windows had grown to real fear now. His headlights swept across the treeline as the driveway curled ahead. He squinted into the woods.

Reaching the end of the drive, he pulled out onto the single lane track that led, after a mile or so, back to the highway. He'd purposely rented a house out of the city; he had no interest in having neighbours, in having to see or speak to anyone anymore. After Alex had been murdered, he and Lucy had tried to cling to some semblance of a normal life. All that had brought them was agony. Now he just wanted to be left alone.

There were no lights along the track and the steel glow of the moon had been smothered by heavy clouds overhead. Matt strained to look into the woods as he drove. All the time the track ahead developed, foot by foot, in the Camaro's headlamps. A huddle of twisted figures, the trunks of oaks, crowded the edge of the dirt road. He cracked the window and the howls were closer now. Were they ahead? Coming from along the track?

Matt drove until the rutted track became the highway. He wound the window tight against the sound and put his foot down. He left the woods behind, his fear beginning to recede as he put more distance between himself and the crying that had woken him. The motion of the car calmed his nerves, the repetition of the road lulling him towards sleep. He thought he was driving without direction, letting the road take him away from whatever stalked the woods. He was wrong.

The sound found him. It cut between the growling of the Camaro's engine—a startling, mournful wail. Matt stood on the brakes. The car swerved to a stop, the front end veering into the oncoming lane. Had he been asleep? He killed the engine. The V8 wound down and stopped. The headlights blinked out.

Matt sat in the darkness.

A stillness descended on the Camaro.

When it came again, the sound made him cry out. How could it have followed him? He'd driven for miles. Surely anything so badly injured couldn't have kept pace all this way? It came again, louder now, closer than it had been on the dirt track.

Matt spun, squinting into the dark behind him. The tree-lined road seemed empty. Another cry cut through the night air. Matt's body was tight, he snatched for the key to start the Camaro. He twisted back to face the front...then he saw it.

On the edge of the trees, just before the wet asphalt disappeared into the night, a sign leaned out towards the road. Matt recognized it straight away. He'd seen it before, on the night Alex had died. A few months before, two teenagers had run off the road and into the sign. It'd buckled over the hood of their car. The car was long gone, but the sign, bent over like an old man on the side of the highway, remained. On the night of Alex's disappearance, he'd driven this road searching the treeline for any sign of his son. From a distance he'd mistaken the sign for someone standing on the edge of the road. He'd slowed as he'd passed, just long enough to see the wilting flowers that had been placed at the foot of the sign. He'd started to cry, overwhelmed by a terrible sense of the inevitable.

Matt thought he'd been driving away from the sound.

He'd been driving towards it.

It would draw him all the way to 1428 Montgomery.

The wailing grew louder, clearer with every mile he drove. He gripped the wheel, pleading for it to stop. He could tell now that it wasn't a dying animal: it was a human cry, horribly distorted. They were Alex's cries, terrified and in agony, screaming for someone, *anyone*, to help him. They were the cries he should have heard on that awful April night, the sound he should have followed to the black house to help his son.

Matt drove too fast on the wet asphalt. He called to Alex, trying to soothe his pain but the awful mewling just grew louder as it pulled him through the night.

Montgomery was still, deaf to Alex's suffering. Matt threw the Camaro up onto the curb and ran for the house. He tore across the overgrown lawn. In his heart he knew it couldn't be real, knew that Alex was gone, but still he could hear his son, *he could hear him screaming*! He jumped up onto the porch and ran for the door.

"I'm here, son! I'm here! Daddy's here! It's okay! It's going to be okay!" The moment Matt touched the front door, the screaming stopped. "No! Alex! Alex!" He barged against the door, slamming against it. "Alex, please!"

No answer came.

Matt threw himself against the door, again and again, trying to break it in, trying to get to Alex.

But Alex was gone.

"I'm sorry! Alex! I'm so sorry!"

Matt fell against the door and wept.

The scream jolted Matt awake. Immediately he was back, standing outside 1428 Montgomery on that July night. *The screaming was Alex's—rising from what remained of his blasted-apart throat, blood choking his terrified cries.* The screaming was Matt's cell phone drumming angrily on the bedside table. *Matt slammed against the door, trying to beat it down, trying to get to Alex.*

He fumbled for the phone and answered it. In the thick darkness, the nightmare of the night outside 1428 Montgomery clung to him. Matt grabbed for the bedside lamp and flicked it on. He was shaking. It was 4:00am.

"Hello?" Matt's voice was rough, hoarse from crying out to Alex in his sleep.

The laugh that replied almost made him drop the phone. The sound was barely human. The breathing that followed was heavy, fast.

"Who is this?" The night seemed to draw tighter around him. He moved closer to the dim light of his bedside lamp.

"I've seen it!" the voice screamed. Then it was laughing, madness pulled taut, soaked in sweat and terror. Matt's blood turned to ice. He knew the voice. Knew it but barely recognized it.

Lucy's mouth was pressed against the receiver; Matt could feel her frenzied breathing pulsing in his ear. One moment her voice was barely a whisper, the next screaming, out of control, as if two entities fought to control the same mouth.

"Fuck! They use their bones to cut their flesh. Split and grind. Fuck the open wounds. Fuck the open wounds. Deep, deep, pushing, thrusting into the sticky meat!"

"Lucy? Lucy? What's going on?"

Could she even hear him? Matt had once seen a woman speaking in tongues in a church. Lucy's rambling, muttering and then screaming reminded him of that.

"I've seen the place, in the messages! The place where he is. It's horrible!

The old ones. The oldest ones! They've been there forever. They're insane. They're all insane. So many bodies. Torn apart. There are children there!"

"Lucy, listen to me, it's okay. Can you hear me, Lucy? What you're saying, it's not real."

"No! It's where they all go. Don't you understand? The madness infects them all. They're fucked, they're all fucked!"

Then she was laughing again, strained and painful, as if each bark forced itself up through her throat, rough and hard.

"Are you fucking listening to me you cunt? They feed on the weak, wear their fucking skins! Hide! HIDE! I can smell the blood! So much blood! Slit you up the middle, see it all spill out, faster, faster, faster, faster, yellow fat in my hands, in my mouth."

Matt couldn't listen to any more. "Stop! Lucy! Lucy, please! Stop! You've got to stop this!"

The line went quiet.

"Lucy? Are you there?"

Lucy's breathing came close to the phone once more. She was crying.

"Make it stop. Please make it stop," she pleaded. The line went dead.

31

NEVER OVER

Matt sat on the edge of his bed, circled by darkness and silence. Both felt charged, as if they somehow teemed with the terrible things Lucy had described. As if they'd slithered out of her mouth and into the reality of his room. He'd known Lucy for more than ten years, and even when she'd been at her lowest, her most broken—before she'd checked herself into the hospital—he could never have imagined her saying the things he'd just heard.

What she'd described was pure madness. He couldn't get the images out of his head. He got up and crossed the bedroom to the light switch, slamming his hand down on it, flooding the room with bright light. The thick shadows that had crowded his bed were chased back into the corridor. The silence remained behind, though. And it was filled with whispering: Lucy's words, repeating over and over.

Matt realized he was still gripping his phone. He wanted it to ring again, for Lucy to be at the other end of the line reassuring him she was okay, that it had been some kind of night terror, a fever dream. At the same time, he dreaded it ringing again, dreaded what might be waiting for him when he answered.

When he'd found Lucy at the house he'd been heartbroken, sickened by what she'd done. But he didn't blame her. He blamed Bachman. Why had Bachman let her leave the hospital when she was so clearly still consumed by grief? Matt thought she'd been getting better. That's what the doctor had told him. He'd called Bachman, furious, demanding answers; then he'd implored him to do something.

He should have gone back and dragged her out of that evil place himself.

Matt eyed the darkness in the corridor. It seemed to shift and churn as he watched. He snapped the hallway light on to drive it away. Had Lucy been talking about Alex? *The place where he is.* Even the suggestion his little boy could be in the hell Lucy described filled him with a horror that seized around his heart. The same desperate helplessness he'd felt that night outside 1428 Montgomery.

Matt moved from room to room until he'd switched on every light in his house.

32

It looked down at Lucy, unconscious on the cold boards of *his* room. It had watched her before, watched her for hours, studied every detail of her—the way her pale skin pulled taut over her bones, veins bulging fat just beneath the surface. She had locked herself away, cut her ties with the outside world, wasted away until she was a dead thing calling to the dead. They had answered.

It had watched as the blood flowed freely from the wound on her forehead. Watched as it clotted in black stars through her matted hair. Stood over her as it slowly congealed to a sticky red mouth just below her hairline.

Now, it held her hand, its small decayed fingers wrapped around Lucy's. Its grip was terribly cold, wet, the flesh loose on its bones. Its wrist had disappeared completely where its arm had decomposed and bloated. The skin on its forearm had sloughed off, revealing the blackened, putrefying muscle beneath. Further up the arm the body had been—

Lucy stirred. Her eyes flickered open. She squinted into the darkness above her.

She was alone. But, no—she'd felt something—someone had been in the room with her!

"Alex?" Lucy rolled on to her side. The pain brought her to a dead stop. It exploded behind her eyes, making her cry out. Her skull felt vice tight, too full, full of blood? She could taste it in her mouth.

The night came back to her in a sickening wave, *his* Ouija board message, the black thing that tore out of the darkness at her. She raised an unsteady hand up towards her head. That was when she saw the plaster dust.

Her fingers were covered in it. Plaster dust and blood. Where the child had been holding her hand, her fingers were bleeding. Lucy ran her other hand over the tiny cuts on her fingers. She winced, blood streaking through the white dust.

"Alex?" she called quietly. The house remained silent and still.

Lucy turned onto her front. Her movement made the pain surge horribly, the pressure in her head ratcheting up until it felt like it would burst. She planted her hands on the stripped boards and slowly managed to haul herself up onto all fours. All the time she could hear herself whimpering, but the voice sounded distant, disconnected from her, as if she was listening to the suffering of someone else in the room with her.

She crawled across the floor to the wall by the bedroom door. There, leaning into the wall for support, she managed to pull herself to her feet. The pain made her eyes blur with tears. She couldn't give up now. She mustn't! She'd felt Alex, felt him holding her hand. Her Alex! Finally, after everything she'd endured, she was close, so close to seeing him again. But she was freezing, as cold as the house that had swallowed her. It had finally gotten its wish, she thought. She had become one with it.

It was you, *wasn't it,* Alex?

Please don't hide anymore.

Swaying away from the door frame, Lucy pulled herself out of Todd Lowe's room. She stumbled and fell into the wall on the other side of the hallway. Her head was pounding, each beat of her heart was a scream locked tight in her skull. She thought of the black mass that had torn from the night and attacked her. Was it waiting along the corridor for her? Was that what she'd pulled from death with her desperate pleas? Resting her head on the wall, she felt warm blood flowing over her face. As she dragged herself along the wall, she streaked the cream paint red.

"Mommy's here!" Her words were slurred. The world slipped in and out of focus. The wall ended, and Lucy found herself leaning on the bannister for support, sliding along it towards the top of the stairs. When the bannister ran out there was nothing left to hold her up. She stood, swaying over the staircase that dropped away in front of her, tottering on the edge of the top step.

And then she lost her balance.

Lucy swung her arms, pinwheeling wildly, trying frantically to stop herself falling forward. She rocked back, staggered, and managed to propel herself backwards across the landing. Out of control, she spun and slammed into the side of the wardrobe.

She sank to her knees, leaning into the cold wood. She gripped the sides of the hulking box, afraid that if she let go the world would throw her off again.

Lucy knelt against the wardrobe for a long time before she felt strong enough to try and pick herself up. She reached up to the wall beside her. She felt the letters before she saw them.

The plaster behind the wardrobe had been cut into—deep channels, gouging out another message. Lucy turned towards the words.

At the same moment, something began hammering on the inside of the wardrobe.

33

The wardrobe shook, a flurry of blows pummelling the wood, as if something were trying to beat its way out, fighting to get to Lucy. She reeled away, landing awkwardly on her back, elbows slamming into the stripped boards first, her whole body jarring as it followed.

Another peal of blows erupted. Lucy screamed and wriggled away from the sound. She crawled backwards across the landing until the bannisters cut off her retreat.

There she lay, wide-eyed, cornered, waiting for whatever lurked inside the closet to begin thrashing at its sides again.

No more blows came.

Lucy took a grip on the bannisters. She used them to pull herself around, to try to look beyond the ajar wardrobe door. Was it waiting for her, a cadaver coiled into the thick darkness, waiting for her to round the door before tearing into her?

A bit at a time she shifted closer, straining to see past the heavy door. From the angle she was viewing it, she couldn't ignore how much the wardrobe resembled an oversized coffin. Neither could she ignore how that coffin loomed over her, as if it were sizing her up.

As close as she dared to get, Lucy couldn't see clearly around the door. Her face felt numb now, the metallic tang of blood filled her mouth, a bitter reminder of how far she'd come.

Lucy edged along the side of the wardrobe until she was kneeling in the same place she'd been when the knocking began. She raised her hands up to its frame. She stopped, her trembling hands just short of the cold wooden box. She was certain that, as soon as she touched it, the hammering would begin again.

Gently, she placed her hands on the wood.

No sound came from the wardrobe. With one hand underneath it and another gripping the back of its frame, Lucy strained to pull the wardrobe away from the wall. The pain in her head surged. She screamed out, but she couldn't stop, she *wouldn't* stop. The wardrobe felt as if it were full of bricks.

A fresh stream of blood traced a path down Lucy's face. It felt as if the skin on her forehead was tearing, the mouth opening, peeling apart as she strained to drag the dead weight away from the wall. The cuts on her fingers were bleeding again. Her grip was slick with sweat and blood.

The wardrobe scraped loudly on the floorboards. Inch by inch, Lucy hauled it, ever closer to exposing the message. Blood from her fingers smeared the varnish.

And then the wardrobe slipped out of her hands. The sudden release sent Lucy spinning away, she lost her footing and plopped down onto the hallway floor. There, sitting in the hulking shadow of the wardrobe, she read the two word message cut into the wall.

34

ALL WAYS ME

The words were large, jagged, torn with force into the wall.

"What are you trying to say? What does this mean?" Lucy demanded.

She pulled herself to her feet, grabbing the bannister to steady herself. She'd been through the whole house looking for messages, but she hadn't thought to look behind the furniture the Lowes had abandoned. She hadn't thought to pull the pictures from the walls, to tear into the plaster, to carve and cut and rip into it. There were carpets in some of the rooms. There might be messages underneath them! Keeping a tight grip on the bannister, Lucy began to make her way down the stairs.

Each step seemed further away than the last, the drop between them growing larger all the time. The world blurred in and out of focus, her legs could barely hold her up.

She was halfway down the staircase when she heard the noise. It cut through the hallway like a scream: the squeal of wood scoring the floor above her. Lucy whipped around.

The huge shape lumbered into view, grinding loudly on the floor as it moved. It took a moment for Lucy to realize what she was looking at. The wardrobe was being shoved, little by little, towards the top stair.

Lucy stepped fast down the stairs, faster with each scrape from above. She stumbled, jumped down the stairs. Still, she was nowhere near the bottom when the wardrobe reached the top step and, with one final shove, rocked forward and plummeted over the edge.

35

The wardrobe toppled forward, its door swinging wide as it dropped hard onto the staircase. In her panic, Lucy lost her footing and her grip on the bannister. She slipped onto her back and slid down the stairs, the huge mass of the wardrobe hammering after her.

Lucy hit the bottom step moments before the wardrobe. For a split second she saw the massive dark form of the cabinet speeding towards her…and then everything went black.

Lucy's scream was lost in the massive noise of the wardrobe slamming into the wall at the bottom of the staircase, driving into it with such force its sides shattered. The top of the wardrobe embedded itself deep into the plaster.

36

M att grabbed the Camaro's keys from the hall table and headed for the garage. The corridor was freezing. He'd set the heating to run all night, but still the cold had found its way inside. His skin pulled tight against the frigid air. The hallway bulb had blown not long after he'd moved in and he hadn't gotten around to changing it. Now he wished he had.

He couldn't get Lucy's words out of his head. Pacing along the corridor, following the wall through the dark, he felt that, at any moment, the shadows might rush at him, tear into view as one of the grotesque apparitions Lucy had described. He walked faster. Or maybe he would find it, slithering across the tiles, waiting to catch at his ankles, white skin at first, then wet, torn flesh and shattered bone.

They use their bones to cut their flesh.

Matt snatched at the handle to the garage door. Before he'd opened it halfway, his other hand was already searching the wall inside for the light switch. He found it and flicked it on. The fluorescent tube flickered, the same darkness he'd hurried through snatching in between each blink.

Matt shut the door on the hallway. Maybe the door had shifted in the cold, the hinges tightened, but it was harder to close than usual, like closing a door against a strong wind, like something pushed against it from the other side. The darkness swelled against the rippled glass panels in the hallway door.

At the back of the garage was the jerry can Matt had taken to 1428 Montgomery. He should have burned the black house to ashes when he'd had the chance. He grabbed the can and headed around to the Camaro's trunk.

Matt stopped, turning fast to look at the glass panel at the bottom of the hallway door. Had something moved just beyond the glass? He'd caught it on the edge of his peripheral vision—something more than the dark pressing against the pane. He studied the glass, waiting. The corridor beyond seemed still. That did not put his mind at rest.

Matt put the can into the trunk. He had to get Lucy out of that house, put an end to this. He'd trusted Doctor Bachman to help her but he'd done nothing. He slammed the trunk, angry with himself. The noise echoed through the still space, setting the garage door rattling as if someone were beating on it, trying to get in. As Matt climbed into the Camaro he looked back to the rippled glass pane.

He stopped, garage remote in hand, the memory of the night Alex's cries had led him to 1428 Montgomery holding him still. He'd tried to blame his grief, tried to convince himself it had been some kind of hallucination brought on by the insatiable pain of losing Alex. He'd returned to the house, kept watch, but had found only silence beyond its mottled panes. Now he was sure there had been something more, something in the darkness that had lured him there. Had it wanted him to break in, to find it among the shadows and dust? Had it been waiting for Lucy? Drawing her to it the way it had drawn him, with the promise of seeing their son again? Matt's hands were shaking, fear uncoiling within him. He closed his hand around the remote. The door jerked upwards and the night seized its chance to sweep in. Snow swirled under the garage door—the freezing air outside was thick with it. The low, grey winter sky that had been threatening snow for days had finally delivered on its promise.

Matt turned the key in the Camaro's ignition. Its roar made him start. Its headlights blasted into the night, alive with snow spinning through their beams. Matt edged it out of the garage. All around the Camaro, the night shifted and changed shape. Squalls threw themselves against the car like furious ghosts. The heavy fall had already begun to lay. Matt's tires skidded as he pulled onto the drive. The roads would be treacherous, but he had no choice. He had to get Lucy out of 1428 Montgomery before it was too late.

37

Matt could barely feel the wheel. He'd turned the heating up full, hot air blasted from the vents on the dashboard, his face felt flushed and raw, but still he couldn't rid himself of the biting cold that had lingered at his back ever since he had gotten into the Camaro. Snow crowded the windshield. As quickly as the blades of his wipers could cast it aside, it swarmed out of the night again. Matt knew he was driving too fast. He had to get to Lucy.

38

Lucy lay on the landing at the bottom of the stairs. The massive shape of the wardrobe loomed over her. For the second time that night she thought how much it resembled a coffin.

It was a fluke she hadn't been crushed. The wardrobe had slammed into the wall at the bottom of the staircase with such force it had wedged itself between the wall and the bottom step. It hung a few inches above her.

The sides of the wardrobe shifted and groaned, the last breaths of a dying animal. She could hear the wood splintering under its own weight.

Behind Lucy's head, the plaster in the wall crumbled and the huge mass of the closet jolted closer to her. She screamed, her cry echoing into the stale blackness that filled the wardrobe. In the fall, the door had swung wide. Now she was face to face with the darkness she'd tried to look into upstairs. It was stagnant, pitch, she could almost feel it pressing against her. Inside the wardrobe, something moved.

Lucy caught her breath and held it. She tried to stifle her terrified whimpering, as if somehow her silence might hide her. Something she couldn't see shifted inside the dark space, sliding, moving towards her.

She panicked. She squirmed back, trying to pull away, to wriggle out from under the wardrobe. The instant she shifted, the pain exploded in her ankle. The remains of the smashed wardrobe door had pinned her leg to the ground. Each time she tried to pull away, the door bit deeper into her flesh. Each time she tried to pull away the pain was a white-hot shock that made her cry out.

Something fell against the inside of the wardrobe. Right on the edge of the darkness now.

Lucy grabbed a hold of the wardrobe door. She tried to shake it, to force it off her leg. Behind her she could hear the plaster in the wall cracking with each shake. At any moment the wardrobe might break free of the wall, all of its weight collapsing onto her. The door would rip through her ankle, splintered wood severing her foot before the weight of the wardrobe crushed her.

Lucy stopped. Something was watching from the darkness suspended above her.

Suddenly a bone, stripped of flesh, jagged and sharpened, tore out of the black. It slammed into the landing, driven into the boards by Lucy's head. Lucy screamed. She ripped at her trapped leg. With every jerk the door knifed deeper into her ankle, splintered wood gouging into the flesh. The bone slithered back inside the wardrobe.

Desperate to free herself, Lucy twisted her body, driving her shoulder into the landing, reaching across herself until she was able to grip the side of the wardrobe with both hands. She pulled with all her strength.

The wardrobe door cracked loudly, its jagged edge peeling back the skin from her ankle. Her screams filled the hallway.

The splintered wood jammed on Lucy's ankle bone. She tried to twist her foot, to wriggle free. It was like sliding her ankle across a razor blade. The pain blurred the world around her. The stinking darkness above began to spill out of the wardrobe, as if it were reaching out to smother her. She was blacking out from the pain. If she didn't get free soon, she'd pass out.

Her fingers were slippery with sweat and blood. She dug them into the edge of the wardrobe and hauled. The wardrobe groaned, the door grinding on her ankle bone. The harder she pulled, the tighter it gripped her.

"Alex! Help me! Please!"

With a sickening crack, bones snapping, Lucy tore her leg free. She dragged herself out from underneath the wardrobe and slid down the last steps onto the hallway floor. She lay on the cold floor, whimpering and broken, blood from her useless foot streaking a trail behind her. She tried to pull herself up, but the pain threw her screaming to her knees.

Lucy heard the bone slam into the landing behind her. She twisted back to see a black shape spill from the wardrobe, a terrible mass of limbs birthed from its dark wooden womb.

Lucy grabbed at the hallway floor, hand over hand she dragged herself away from the thing. She could hear it advancing, tumbling down the stairs and onto the floor behind her.

She was moving too slow! She slapped her hands down to the boards and hauled herself as fast as she could towards the first door that came out of the night at her.

She dragged herself through the living room door and slammed it shut.

39

L ucy sat against the living room door, bracing against it as best she could from her crumpled position on the floor. *What was that thing? What was that thing?* She'd only caught a glimpse of it—black limbs unfurling in the darkness, but she knew it had come for her. She knew she had to get out of the house. *Now!*

The night had closed like a fist around her. It was thick with the sound of her blood rushing in her ears, with the blasting of her ragged breathing. How could she tell where *it* was if she couldn't hear it over her own panic?

She shifted against the door. The slightest movement made her want to scream out in agony. She clamped a hand over her mouth to cover the sound of her crying. Even in the dim light of the living room she could see that her foot twisted away from her leg at an angle that was awkward and wrong. She wouldn't be able to run when it came for her.

Lucy pressed her ear to the living room door. To *one* of the living room doors. She'd slammed this one closed on the thing. On the other side of the room, the second door was wide open.

40

Lucy listened at the door, trying to make out any noise from the hallway. Where was it? The house had fallen silent.

Behind Lucy, on the other side of the room, pieces of the shattered mirror specked the floor, a thousand dead stars reflecting only darkness. Long shadows stretched onto the living room wall like doorways to unthinkable realms. Another message had been scored into the plaster.

SAME FOR ALL

Did something move against the wall?

Lucy reached up for the doorknob. It was freezing. Unnaturally cold. Was the black thing waiting for her on the other side of the door? Its terrible form coiled in the hallway, biding its time, waiting for a chance to drive that sharpened bone into her flesh?

She had no choice. She had to get out of the house! That meant going through the hallway.

No! She couldn't do it! She couldn't turn the handle, face the horror that stalked the house. She leaned against the door, her fear too strong. Behind her the darkness swelled, thick and fluid.

She *had* to get out of the house. Maybe, if she stuck to the very edges of the hall, clung to the darkest parts of the room, she might be able to make it to the front door unseen.

If she didn't move, it would stalk her.

If she didn't move, it would find her.

She could already smell its stench on the air.

What had she done?

Get out, Lucy! Get out now!

Bracing against the door, in case the thing charged it, Lucy began to turn the handle.

41

The door shifted in its frame. The movement made Lucy start; a small, frightened cry escaped her lips. It was swallowed into the vast blackness of the hallway. Had she given herself away? Had it heard her?

She shuffled backwards, little by little pulling the living room door towards her, until she was able to see around it into the hallway. She stayed behind the door, sheltering behind it, as she looked across to the staircase and the remains of the wardrobe.

The hallway was still. It seemed deserted. Nothing moved near the wardrobe, and the space beneath it seemed empty. Where had it gone?

Lucy pulled the door open further, edging round it until there was no barrier between her and whatever might lurk in the hall.

Oh, God, please don't let it see me!

Trailing her shattered foot behind her, Lucy began to pull herself forward, out from her hiding spot. As she rounded the door's frame she snatched a look towards the front door.

It had curled into the shadows against the living room wall, underneath the words it had gouged. Now the shadows shifted: the thing began to move along the cold plaster.

The bone hit the ground and began to carve. The floorboards screeched as it scraped along the wood, scoring into the living room floor the way it had torn into the walls of the house.

Lucy spun to the noise. Utterly terrified, she fell onto her back. She'd only made it halfway through the living room door. Although her mind screamed for her to flee, to haul herself away, her body had stopped listening to her.

No! Not now! Please!

Move! MOVE!

Paralysed by her fear, Lucy could only listen to the sound of the bone screeching across the floor as, inch by inch, it gained on her.

42

Matt leaned forward in his seat, trying to pull the road ahead from the snow swarming in his headlights. The Camaro's wipers arced back and forth, a futile attempt to sweep the endless drifts from the windscreen. The downfall had grown heavier with every mile. He knew he was driving too fast—driving blind—but he had to get to Lucy. He didn't realize he'd drifted into the oncoming lane.

43

High beams tore out of the storm, headed straight for the Camaro. Matt jerked hard on the wheel.

It was already too late for the other driver to change course.

The Camaro swerved, skidding on the frozen road.

For a moment the snow was on fire, ash swirling in a firestorm. It was terrible, and somehow strangely beautiful. *This is the last thing I'll ever see,* thought Matt.

Please, God, let me see Alex again.

Glass exploded, metal sheared apart. The wing mirrors of the two cars clipped and were torn off. Their bodies roared past each other, inches from colliding. The wail of the other driver's horn was swallowed into the white and gone.

The Camaro kept skidding.

Matt slammed on the brakes, but the car hit the barrier, the edge of the road overlooking the bay.

Metal ground on metal, the Camaro bucking against the guard rail as if it were looking for a way through. Matt fought to get the car under control, the wheel shook so violently he could barely hold onto it. The barrier screamed along the side of the car. But it held, and Matt managed to wrestle the Camaro back onto the road.

His hands were bleeding, rubbed raw by the wheel. His driver's side headlamp had blown out. None of that mattered. Matt put his foot down again. He had to get to Lucy.

44

Death had come for Lucy. She had hauled it from the black with her pleas, a monster made of tears, wrapped in the dead skin of her grief. She had created it and now it was going to kill her.

The bone carved deep into the wooden floor, corkscrews of peeled wood trailing behind it as it gained on her. Soon that would be her flesh. It was over. She would never see Alex again.

She started to sob. Not from fear, but because she'd truly believed she'd contacted Alex, that it was him holding her hand in Todd Lowe's room, that, after everything she'd endured, she could have seen her broken, beautiful boy once more.

Please don't let it end like this!

She fought to break free of her paralysis, her mind screaming at her motionless body. From where she lay, she could see her hands, streaked in blood and plaster dust, useless at her sides.

Closer, ever closer. Now she could feel the bone's approach vibrating through the boards beneath her.

MOVE!

PLEASE MOVE!

If she died now, she'd leave Alex in the darkness. Scared and alone. If she died now, she'd fail him again. Just as she had nine months before.

Like a shadow come alive, the black thing rounded the corner of the wall. Lucy could feel the cold pouring from it.

"NO! NO! NO!" she screamed. She wouldn't fail Alex again. In that instant her paralysis was gone. She threw her hands out to her sides and gripped onto the living room door frame. She shoved hard, propelling herself backwards, across the floor and out into the hallway. There, she rolled onto her front. She couldn't run, her broken foot wouldn't take her weight. So, she grabbed at the hallway floor and pulled with all the strength her exhausted, broken body had left. She dragged herself inch by excruciating inch across the cold boards.

The bone scoring the floor grew closer.

Lucy hauled herself towards the front door.

The message carved into the wood of the door stopped her in her tracks.

45

Don'T LEeve mOMMY

Lucy shook her head. It couldn't be. It couldn't be! She raised a hand to her mouth but the words had already escaped: "Always me."

She couldn't take them back.

A cry tore from Lucy's lips. Even muffled by her hand, it was a terrible sound. A wail of pure mad grief. Everything she'd seen and been through, suddenly made a dreadful, unthinkable sense. She understood! She understood what he'd been trying to tell her.

"Oh no! No, no, no…" She choked the words through her sobbing. She hadn't ever been talking to the kidnapper. The messages, the horrific, insane messages. They'd been Alex all along. Not the Alex she'd lost on that terrible night in April but what remained of a boy thrown into the barbaric place she'd witnessed when she'd been unconscious.

Same for all.

She couldn't believe it. She refused to believe it. It was too cruel, too black, too much for her heart to bear.

The sound of the bone gouging the floor had stopped. Lucy could feel the presence behind her.

46

YOUR MONSTER

The Camaro sped through the storm. For a moment everything was still. Silent. As if the night had drawn its breath…

Lucy pulled herself to her knees. She wasn't running any more. She felt the slick cold press against her. The stench of decomposition, of liquifying flesh, closed around her. A bloated hand slithered under her arm and, on the other side, a sharpened bone, cut from the stump of an arm, pressed into her side. Alex's corpse hugged his mother's back.

And the night screamed. The storm roared around the Camaro. The momentary silence was gone. In the same instant, Matt felt the Camaro lose power. The engine wound down, the car skidded across the road, sliding, losing speed the whole time.

"No! No! Not now!"

Matt pumped the gas but nothing happened. Then all the lights on the dashboard blinked out.

Matt twisted the key in the ignition again and again. Nothing. The Camaro was dead. He slammed his fist on the steering wheel. Something was terribly wrong with Lucy. He was sure of it. He didn't stop to think. He ditched the Camaro and began to run through the storm to Lucy.

Lucy turned to face the remains of her son. "It's okay… It's okay, Mommy's here. Mommy's here now. I…I didn't understand. I'm so sorry." Lucy put her arms around the corpse and hugged it to her. "I thought I'd lost you! I thought I'd lost you forever! I'm so sorry. I won't leave. It's okay. You don't have to worry. I promise, I won't leave you again. I won't leave you again." A swollen child's hand and the sharpened bone dug into Lucy's back, gripping her tightly.

Matt stopped. His breath tore from his body in smoking blasts. The storm circled him, surrounding him instantly, blinding white on all sides. He crumpled—a sickening sense that he was too late ripping the fight from him.

47

The truck driver found Matt by the side of the road. Half frozen, raving about his wife and 1428 Montgomery. He gave Matt his jacket, turned the heating up full blast. He offered to drive him to the hospital. That's where he should have been heading in his state. But Matt went half crazy at that idea. Instead, he drove him out to the house.

Matt sprinted across the weed-choked lawn, just as he'd done on the night the screaming had lured him to the house. The snow had hit the city proper now, the freezing air was thick with it. He skidded over the icy boards of the porch and slammed against the front door.

"Lucy! Lucy!" he yelled, right up to the door, trying to listen for any noise as she shouted. "It's Matt! Are you in there? Can you hear me?"

He hammered frantically.

"Lucy, please! Let me in!"

Nothing. He had to get inside!

Matt kicked at the door. He knew he wasn't strong enough to force it. He'd tried that the last time. He rushed back down on to the frozen lawn.

He could barely see through the tumbling snow, but he could just make out the right bedroom window. He watched it, looking for movement, a figure, any sign someone had heard him.

"LUCY!" He cupped his hands and called again.

He knew that was Todd Lowe's room. He knew every room in the house. He'd learned their layout the same way Lucy had. He'd read all of her cuttings, every terrible word of them. He knew that if Lucy was in the house, she'd likely be in that room.

Matt stepped backwards. His heel caught on a pile of snow-covered bricks and he almost went over. Ted had been building Anna a vegetable garden before they'd abandoned the house. Matt bent down and picked up one of the bricks.

The living room window exploded inwards. The storm followed it in. The brick caught in the heavy curtains and dropped to the boards with a muffled thud. Matt pushed the rest of the shattered glass out of the frame and clambered inside. Snow swarmed after him.

"LUCY! Lucy, are you here?"

Matt hurried across the lounge, the electric dread that coursed through him flaring to full-blown panic when he saw the track carved into the floorboards.

"Oh my God, Lucy!" He broke into a run.

When he hit the hallway, he spotted the shattered wardrobe on the landing at the bottom of the staircase. He saw the trail of black liquid spilling over the stairs and down onto the boards.

"Oh no! No!"

He didn't think, he didn't stop to look around the hallway. He raced across the room to the wardrobe. He fumbled underneath it, grabbing for a handhold. As his fingers skirted the shattered wood around the door, he noticed the smell. Metal? Blood? He could taste it on the freezing air. He found an edge and gripped it, reaching into the darkness that had borne a monster.

48

Matt's arms shook, splintered wood cut deep into his fingers. He strained to lift the weight of the wardrobe from the floor. He could hear wood cracking, splitting apart. He heaved the closet up, adrenaline giving him the strength to make the final push and tip the wardrobe onto its side against the wall.

Lucy wasn't under the wardrobe. *Thank God.* But now Matt could see the extent of the black liquid, could see how it was smeared all over the landing, how it seemed to have spilled from the broken wardrobe, as if the darkness itself had come alive. Just how he'd feared the shadows in his house might. Something white, in the farthest corner of the wardrobe's insides, caught Matt's attention. He leaned in towards the doorway.

A startling creak from the crumbling frame almost sent him reeling backwards. He grabbed a hold of the edge of the doorway to steady himself. The wardrobe groaned again. It wouldn't be able to support its own weight much longer. Matt looked into the darkness. The stench from inside the closet was overpowering now. It was blood. Blood and rot. It caught in his throat and made him gag. Turning his face away, he reached blind into the black.

He reached in until his shoulder leaned against the frame, until his whole arm was swallowed into the wardrobe. His fingers swept through the fetid air. Then they fell upon the white shape.

It was wet. Paper. He closed his hand around it and peeled it from the corner of the wardrobe. As he pulled the book toward him, he caught a glimpse of its cover. At the same moment there was a startling crack, and the wardrobe finally collapsed. The top and bottom gave way, and the two sides of the closet fell on one another like a giant jaw snapping shut.

Matt snatched his hand away just as the mouth closed tight. He stumbled back across the landing, the copy of the BFG he'd retrieved from the ruined wardrobe dripping with the putrid fluid that had been smeared across the boards at his feet. It was Alex's copy. His favorite book. He'd written his name in the front of it. But it was barely recognizable. The pages had been torn into, shredded. It was falling apart in Matt's hands. He cradled it in his fingers, trying to hold it together.

"Oh God, Lucy, what have you done?"

Matt turned to the staircase.

"LUCY? LUCY?"

Please answer me!

His calls were met with silence.

Matt raced up the stairs.

49

His boots were still wet from the snow, and slick from the stinking fluid he'd trodden through on the landing. Matt's feet skidded over the steps as he ran. When he saw the words carved into wall, he was so startled that he stopped dead mid-step.

ALL WAYS ME

The letters were hacked down to the brick. Matt suddenly felt terribly small and vulnerable. How could this have happened? Had Lucy done this? Had someone, some *thing* else gouged out the words? His feet rocked on the edge of the stair where he'd stopped. Nervously, he glanced behind him, back down to the remains of the wardrobe. He'd rushed into the house, desperate to help Lucy, but now he felt like an animal lured into a trap.

Matt threw out a hand for the handrail. He grabbed at it and clung on. This was the place where Alex had been murdered. Where all their lives had ended. A clapboard cadaver where grief inhabited every room. He'd tried to destroy it before, and he'd failed. He'd underestimated its power, and now it closed its black fingers around his heart.

"Where are you, Lucy?" His voice was quiet, scared.

Matt pulled himself up the last few stairs and into the corridor. He knew where the house was leading him, knew he had to go for Lucy's sake, but this was the place where his nightmares took him, and he wasn't sure if he was strong enough to face what lay ahead.

He followed the wall, his apprehension growing with every step.

Please, Lucy, say something!

End this, don't make me do this!

His fingers grazed another message cut into the wall. He snatched his hand away.

SKINNED FACES WATCHING

Too soon he was at the door to Todd Lowe's room.

The door was ajar.

Matt closed his eyes as he pushed the door open.

50

Dawn light had begun to dilute the darkness in Todd Lowe's room. It fell softly upon Alex's broken toys, the paper of his books, his clothes, all stacked neatly in the remains of his case. Carefully packed away by Lucy's feet.

Lucy lay in the middle of the room, Alex's favorite sweater resting under her head as a pillow. She lay with her back to the door.

"Lucy?" Slowly, Matt crossed the room.

Lucy's arms were outstretched in front of her. She had sliced her wrists. Blood pooled under her body, spreading a black outline, pouring into the boards beneath her.

Matt rounded Lucy's body. Her eyes were open, staring ahead. In death she looked content, even happy. The knife she'd used to cut her wrists lay by her side.

Matt sat down on the floor next to his wife. He knew she was gone, her broken heart had finally stopped beating. Nine months ago, they had all died in this room. Everything that had come after had been purgatory.

Lucy had died reaching out. One of her hands was half closed. It held a plaster dust hand print. She'd held her boy's hand as she died. She'd watched Alex as the blood had drained from her body and she'd smiled.

On the edge of the pool of blood, a message had been carved into the wooden floorboards, possibly with the knife that Lucy had used to take her life. It read:

TOGETHER NOW